Praise for *Rotten Be.*

CW00848480

"A fanciful bank robbery in a small-town Southern community entwines a clever British bear as he suffers culture shock. Sweet tea, grits, no hold on the satire. Prepare to be tickled!"

—**Vicki Hendricks**, author of *Fur People*

Praise for *Normal for Norfolk (The Thelonious T. Bear Chronicles)*

"For anyone who's ever wondered what *Paddington at Large* would have been like if it had been written by Raymond Chandler—and who hasn't?—Mitzi Szereto has the answer. Like Philip Marlowe, Szereto's Thelonious T. Bear is a modern knight errant who plays it cool even as the light of suspicion shines on him. And like Paddington, he's short of stature and long on charm. If you like your sleuths tough, cynical and cute as a button, *Normal for Norfolk* is the book for you."

—**Steve Hockensmith**, author of *Holmes on the Range* and *Pride and Prejudice and Zombies: Dawn of the Dreadfuls*

"A rural crime novel I found approachable and engaging, featuring an oddly detached hero who just happens to be a small bear…. I enjoyed my visit to Norfolk and I could certainly *bear* another outing (sorry)!"

—*The American* magazine

"Our tableau involves a bear, you see…and not just any old bear, but a *teddy* bear. Erm, make that a talking (also driving, employed, and somewhat-irritable) teddy bear (yes, *really*, so kindly lower those eyebrows!), positioned as the main character in author Mitzi Szereto's—and writing buddy Teddy Tedaloo's—delightfully quirky spin on the traditional cozy mystery…. I'm looking forward to Thelonious's next big adventure…because after *Normal for Norfolk*, you just know there's gotta be more to come."

—The Literate Kitty

"*Normal for Norfolk* has it all: magic, gritty realism, humor, cultural commentary, intelligence, charm and suspense. The hero of this novel, Thelonious T. Bear, finds himself at the heart of a mystery. He's a photojournalist like no other, a pub-loving, anthropomorphized bear who wears cologne and a deerstalker hat. I am eager to read the next book in Mitzi Szereto's series."

—Janice Eidus, author of *The War of the Rosens* and *The Last Jewish Virgin*

Published by Thelonious T. Bear Books
Thelonious T. Bear Books is an imprint of Midnight Rain Publishing.
www.midnightrainpublishing.com

www.mitziszereto.com
www.teddytedaloo.com

Cover design: Mitzi Szereto and Jorge Finkielman

Publication Data is on file at U.S. Copyright Office, Library of Congress, United States of America.

Prologue

Local Bank Hit by "Animal Dwarf Bandits" with Tommy Guns!
—Front page headline from the *Ferndale Bugle*

RED GEORGIA CLAY.

Staining his fur, sifting down his throat. Its dust coated Thelonious T. Bear's innards like lumpy flour. He imagined being rolled in it and dropped into a pot of boiling oil like the famous Southern fried chicken served at every roadside eatery and small-town diner. A pot of boiling oil couldn't have been much worse than the current air temperature. His fur felt as if it had been pressed with a steam iron, then pressed again.

Thelonious climbed down from the booth of yet another country diner with the omnipresent HOME COOKIN' sign in the window, having just partaken of yet another meal of fried chicken with all the trimmings. Today those trimmings had included fried okra and mashed potatoes along with hush puppies that sat in his belly like lead weights. He'd washed everything down with a large glass of sweet tea that contained so much ice it made his teeth hurt. Thelonious knew he shouldn't have eaten that fried pie for breakfast. Peach, it was. He'd finished it in two bites, hoping the juicy-sweet pastry would provide enough fuel to get him through a few hours' work. But all it did was offer a temporary sugar rush, followed by permanent nausea.

The real American South in all its flag-waving post-Confederate glory—this was what Thelonious planned to chronicle with his camera for his new photojournalism assignment in America. "Think Norfolk, but with peaches!" his publisher Ira Goldfarb had shouted down the phone, his brash Brooklyn accent more fitting a discussion on the merits of pastrami on rye than the particulars of the Deep South. "I want homespun! I want Southern hospitality! I want to smell that fried chicken and taste those grits!"

Grits.

Thelonious gagged at the memory. Grits with butter. Grits with cheese. Grits with shrimp. He'd tried them all, never making it past the first forkful. The texture disgusted him even more than the taste. As for the fried chicken, he'd already smelled enough to last a lifetime. Even his fur smelled like fried chicken.

Placing five American dollars on the table, he toddled toward the diner's exit. "Y'all come back and see us a'gin!" the waitress called out, pocketing the money so quickly Thelonious wondered if it was the first time she'd been given a tip. Well, she deserved it. Aside from the friendly service, she'd offered him a sympathetic ear—and that didn't happen too often.

The night before Thelonious had almost been stung by a scorpion as he stepped into the shower. Scrambling back into his clothes with his fur still wet, he went charging over to the motel's reception desk demanding something be done. Rather than offering an apology, the clerk gawped at Thelonious as if

he'd crawled out of a drain instead of the venomous crea
Although he was eventually given another room, it
located near an ice machine that seemed to be very po]
with guests. It had taken Thelonious so long to fall aslee
missed the 10:00 a.m. check-out. He felt as if he'd br
curfew during wartime as he pleaded his case to the day (
who tried to charge him for an extra night's stay. Thelor
knew it was a stitch-up—and he had no intention of p;
an additional tariff for the privilege of spending another
on scratchy sheets watching bedbugs pole-dancing ar(
him.

To his surprise, Thelonious found himself telling
waitress about his motel misadventure, his voice gruffer
usual and even a bit tearful. "I barely got a wink of sleep
that!" he added, shuddering at the memory of what had
lying in wait for him inside the shower stall.

"Aw, bless your heart!" she cried, patting his paw
pink fingernails like the icing on a cheap birthday cake. "
just set a spell and Ah'll be right back!" The waitress bu
off to the kitchen, returning with a generous slice of p
pie with a scoop of vanilla ice cream on top. "This here
me. Just so's y'all know it ain't *all* bad around here!"

Although the fried version from that morning
remained an undigested wedge of grease inside his]
Thelonious forced himself to eat the pie rather than hur
woman's feelings. By the time he choked down the last
the diner had emptied out except for a leathery-skinnec
codger wolfing down a plate of fried chicken. He
probably one of those "local-yokel" types who'd been coi
in every day for years—the waitress seemed to know
pretty well and someone had even come out of the kit
for a natter.

Thelonious wouldn't have minded taking a few phot(
him, but thought better of it when he noticed how th(
man kept glaring at him. Perhaps he lived in that t
Thelonious had just driven through. The fact that it had
churches plus a bank and a barbecue joint with "shack" i

name was probably all it needed to pass for a bustling metropolis around here. It hadn't looked like the most welcoming of places either. At least a dozen sheriff's deputies had been loitering about on the main street, which seemed odd for an American town so small it probably didn't have its own zip code. Maybe they were bored.

A blast of inhospitable Southern heat slammed into Thelonious as he heaved open the diner's glass door and stepped outside. The bottom edge caught on the heel of one of his trainers as it whooshed shut, leaving an ugly scuff mark. He'd only just bought them too. Thelonious had spent his first official day in America at a retail outlet centre offering designer goods at a discount. Knowing how expensive trainers were back home, he was keen to check out the athletic shops, reckoning he'd make a killing. Instead he struggled to fit his ursine feet into pair after pair, settling for trainers that were too narrow in width and too long in the toe. With luck, they'd stretch out at the sides with wear. The toes he stuffed with loo paper. Provided he didn't run any marathons, they should be fine.

Heat shimmered up from his Mini Cooper, the painted stripes of the Union Jack on the roof rippling like cloth in a breeze. Until now Thelonious had only experienced the occasional English heatwave when electric fans were in short supply and frantic Brits—unused to having their blood boiled—descended on the shops in an end-of-the-world frenzy, fearing they'd melt like ice cream left out in the sun. The electric buzzing of cicadas coming from the Spanish moss made him feel hotter still. Southerners called them *katydids*. Whatever they were, they put up quite a racket.

Tugging his deerstalker hat lower over his furry brow, Thelonious squinted into the blinding sunlight as he lumbered toward the car. He really needed some sunglasses, but he couldn't find any to fit the wide contours of his face. When he'd tried on a pair at the outlet place, he broke a stem. Although the salesperson hadn't made him pay for them and had actually been very nice about it, Thelonious felt so

embarrassed he ended up buying a digital sports watch—and that didn't fit him either.

Between the heat and his overstuffed belly he was ready for a lie-down. Perhaps he'd treat himself to a cosy little B&B tonight instead of another roadside motel, though the last time he'd done that it had cost him three nights' accommodation budget for a one-night stay. Maybe they'd charged extra for the chicken décor. Thelonious couldn't use the toilet without some feathered creature giving him the eye. It reminded him of Baxter House in Norfolk, but at least there it had been the Queen invading his privacy rather than common fowl.

Levering himself up into the Mini's driver's seat with the special pulleys he'd had installed, Thelonious loosened his belt a notch, then tapped on the stereo before returning to the road. He sighed happily as Charlie Parker flushed from his ears the twangy music he'd been forced to listen to at the diner. He'd take the Bird's sax any day over some homage to a pickup truck warbled by a man in a sweaty cowboy hat. Although he had nothing against immersing himself in the Southern experience, there was only so much Southern he could take. A few miles later he came to a large billboard. Its presence was a violation of the bucolic landscape.

HE IS RISEN!

The sign had been splattered with blood—or at least what *looked* like blood. Complementing this simulated gore was an advertisement for a revival meeting for some American Church of God Ministry run by a Pastor Jehoshaphat Jones. It was scheduled to take place in a cheery-sounding hamlet named Repentance. Thelonious had to wonder how much donation money went toward the delivery of Pastor Jones's message to the local population, which consisted of a handful of cows and a vulture pecking at a possum carcass.

Thelonious couldn't resist stopping to photograph the billboard. He even got in a few shots of the vulture, though he used his zoom for those. As he worked, he began to consider the possibilities. A Southern religious revival meeting would make for some interesting content. Despite the fact that he preferred to avoid situations involving large groups of people, he should still try to go. Not liking the way the hungry vulture was eyeing him, Thelonious hurried back to the car and drove off.

The serenity of the countryside was abruptly interrupted as a Georgia State Patrol car came barrelling toward the Mini from the opposite lane, roof lights flashing, siren blaring. The rugged features beneath the trooper's hat were fixed in a determined frown, which shifted into a scowl when he turned to face the Mini Cooper's driver.

Thelonious's gut went into a clench-lock. He wondered if he could be ticketed for driving a right-hand drive vehicle. It was bad enough driving on the wrong side of the road. Every time he got behind the wheel he found himself repeating the mantra *stay on the right, stay on the right*. He decided to take the next turnoff before the state trooper got it into his head to make a U-turn and come after him.

That evening in a motor lodge a few steps up the luxury ladder from the previous night's fleapit, Thelonious tried to relax in the bath. Unfortunately, the television blasting in the adjacent room had other ideas. First it was an advertisement for haemorrhoid relief. Then it was toenail fungus and erectile dysfunction. When another advert followed peddling a medication for vaginal dryness, Thelonious decided he'd had enough. He switched on the taps to full, the sound of running water drowning out humans and their copious maladies. The water also drowned out a breaking news report about a bizarre bank heist that had taken place in Ferndale, the one-horse town he'd driven through earlier that day. Aside from the rather unusual fact that all four robbers were little people who'd been armed with old-fashioned Tommy Guns, they had each worn an animal mask.

One of which was that of a bear.

Chapter One

LIGHTNING FLASHED ACROSS THE ominous grey horizon. Rain hammered the windscreen, sticking like petroleum jelly despite the Mini's hard-working windscreen wipers. One minute Thelonious was being cooked alive, the next he was being drowned.

Trying to find a weather update, he fiddled with the radio tuner until he came to a station with a decent signal, only to end up being treated to another country crooner. This time the song involved a bottle of whiskey. Either these singers all sounded alike or this was the same fellow he'd heard at the diner—the one in love with his pickup truck. After listening through an interminably long advertisement for a church ministry at another station, Thelonious found himself being chastised by an overwrought speaker more concerned about hell and damnation than peril on the highway. As if on cue, a loud crack of thunder shook the Mini.

Thelonious could barely see the taillights of the pickup truck in front of him. Suddenly it braked, causing him to slam his wide flat foot down onto the Mini's built-up brake pedal. The little car went into a fishtail. Thelonious's paws gripped the steering wheel so hard he heard the cartilage pop, the baritone blare of a horn from a lorry driving too fast in the adjacent lane sending his heartbeat into the danger zone. Finally he regained control. Using more caution than a doddering granny stepping into the crosswalk of a busy intersection, he switched lanes to pass the pickup, which now created an even bigger hazard by slowing to a crawl.

A stained mattress stood upright in the truck's open back, ready to flip over onto the highway. Thelonious shook his furry head. If it wasn't furniture it was logs, lumber or steel tubing stacked aiming outward like missiles ready to take down the enemy. As he passed the pickup, he dispatched an angry growl through the rain-slicked window at the driver, whose features were hidden by a thick beard and a trucker hat. Thelonious hoped the man wouldn't get behind him and tailgate—something that seemed to be as common in the South as the unsafe transportation of household goods on public roadways. It was madness trying to drive in this weather. The next exit with a motel and he was out of here.

The prospect of somewhere new had been the main appeal. When the offer had come in to do a photography book on the American South, Thelonious had accepted immediately, barely reading his contract or the fine print pertaining to his allowable expenses. In hindsight he wished he'd negotiated the terms, but he'd been desperate to get out of the shabby bedsit he'd been living in after his post-Norfolk trip to the continent. He hadn't made it much farther than the port of Rotterdam before he realised how silly he was being and returned to British shores. By then the authorities already knew who was responsible for the murders of those village publicans in Norfolk. Thelonious T. Bear was officially in the clear.

Although his travel allowance covered the cost of a hire

car, it did not cover the cost of a trans-Atlantic shipment of a personal vehicle, not even if said vehicle had been modified for the driver's special physical needs. Thelonious had checked every car hire company with locations in Georgia, but all they could offer were minivans for the disabled—and even these were impossible to come by. Well, Thelonious didn't want to drive a minivan, thank you very much. And he wasn't disabled—he was simply small in stature! He needed his Mini Cooper, especially since he planned to stay for a while after he'd completed his assignment. America was a big country—he wanted to explore it. Besides, it wasn't as if he had anything to hurry home to other than a mouldy storage unit in north London.

Although there were plenty of billboards on the interstate, those promising a bed for the night now seemed to be in short supply. Instead billboards for church ministries competed with billboards for porn emporiums offering free truck parking, free coffee and "live" nude dancers. Thelonious was pretty sure he knew who'd win *that* contest. Suddenly he saw an exit sign—and it listed a choice of accommodations, not to mention fast-food joints and restaurant chains serving fare certain to add extra flab to his midsection. "Yes!" he cheered, raising a fisted paw into the air. One of those all-day breakfasts would go down a right treat. Better still, a plate heaped with buttered samphire fresh from the Norfolk tidal marshes. Though the last time Thelonious had described it to a waitress in the hope that something similar could be had here, she'd brought him a bowl of something she called "greens." The stuff was green all right, and probably tasty if you liked tangled bits of grass boiled in salty water.

Thelonious merged onto the busy connector road leading to the motels and eateries, one of which was a waffle emporium that covered the region like horse dung on a stable floor. He gazed longingly toward the car park, which was almost full. He could visualise all the happy diners inside chowing down on their stacks of waffles and their bacon and eggs and hash browns. As he debated whether to join them, the rain came down even harder, slashing diagonally across the Mini's windscreen and forming deep pools along the edges of the roadway. A line of vehicles materialised behind him as they too, fled the interstate. At this rate he might not be able to find a room, especially if he stopped off to eat. Rather than risk it, Thelonious pulled into the driveway of the first motor lodge he came to, cringing when a speed bump scraped the Mini's underside. The only empty parking spaces within easy reach of the lobby were those reserved for the disabled. Maybe he should've rented one of those specially modified minivans after all? At least he'd always be guaranteed the best parking.

The clerk at reception was busy on the telephone. He cast a suspicious eye on Thelonious as he came clanging into the lobby with his suitcase, camera bag and folding metal stepladder, which he'd secured to the suitcase with a bungee cord while standing in the bucketing rain. Water from his deerstalker hat trickled beneath his shirt collar, forming a torturous line down his back and sneaking under the waistband of his trousers. Propping his dripping suitcase against the reception desk, Thelonious clambered up onto it and attempted to make eye contact with the clerk, who seemed determined to ignore him. A white plastic nametag pinned to one dandruff-specked navy-blue lapel read ZEKE.

Thelonious cleared his throat, hoping the motor lodge's employee would take the hint and serve him.

"Yep. That was some tornado we had this mornin'," Zeke said into the phone, continuing to take no notice of the new arrival. "Wife says it done took the neighbour's roof clear off. Ah guess the good Lord was watchin' over us. Even the chickens is fine, though the coop'll need fixin'."

"Excuse me, but I'd like a room!" Thelonious's growly voice sounded gruff even to his own ears, but there wasn't a lot he could do about it. Most of his kind hadn't even mastered the art of speech yet.

Zeke gestured with a thumb toward the clock on the wall

behind him. "Check-in ain't till three."

They were a whopping fourteen minutes shy of the hour. "But it's nearly three now!"

The clerk stared at Thelonious with pink-rimmed eyes. "Ah gotta go," he grumbled into the receiver before banging it down. "Y'all got a reservation?"

"Not exactly."

Removing a pen from a pen cup holder on the countertop, Zeke used it to dig around inside one of his protruding ears, then returned it to the cup for the next lucky employee or customer to use. Thelonious had a sudden mental image of the clerk sitting up in a tree plucking on a banjo. He hoped the rooms came equipped with good security bolts on the doors.

"Either y'all got one or not. So which is it?"

"No. I don't have a reservation."

"Then Ah need to see if we got any rooms left. Thare's a big fah-works display in town tonight. Folks comin' from all over to see it."

"*Fireworks?* In *this* weather?"

Zeke nodded. "Restaurant's full up on dinner reservations too, so y'all won't be able to git in to eat."

The "restaurant" to which Zeke referred was a small coffee shop located off the lobby—and not a very appealing one at that. It looked like the sort of place that served tinned soup but called it "homemade" because it came with a mass-produced bread roll and a pat of margarine instead of the usual packets of Saltines. Thelonious reckoned he'd be better off taking his chances with the waffle restaurant or getting a pizza delivered to his room.

"I'd appreciate your looking," he said, struggling to keep his tone polite. Why did he have to grovel for something he'd be paying good money for?

Zeke pursed his fleshy lips together as if trying to decide whether to check availability or tell the prospective guest, who was dripping water all over the floor, they were fully booked. He spent a long time clacking away on his computer

11

keyboard, his pink eyes darting from the screen to Thelonious, who feared he'd get pneumonia if he had to wait here much longer. The icy blasts of air conditioning from the ceiling vents were chilling him to the bone. The motor lodge should've had a health-warning sign posted by the entrance.

"Looks like y'all's in luck. Ah got a room ready to go. Last one, too!"

"I'll take it!"

"Oh. Just so's y'all know, it's a suite. So it's gonna cost a little more."

"A *suite*? But I don't need a suite!"

"'Fraid it's all Ah got. Take it or leave it."

"Fine, whatever." At this point Thelonious would've agreed to a storage cupboard had it been on offer.

Zeke leaned over the counter to give Thelonious the once-over, his expression indicating that he didn't much like what he saw. "It's on the first floor."

Handing over his credit card, Thelonious filled in the registration form he'd been given, hoping he wasn't using the same pen the clerk had used to clean out his ear hole. Between that monsoon he'd driven through and the aggro over a room, he was so stressed that he forgot the first floor in America was actually the *ground* floor. Therefore he had a wasted trip struggling up the stairs with his burdens before discovering that the room numbers began with *2*, whereupon he had to drag everything downstairs again. Thelonious felt a right mug as he clattered back into the lobby, his ill-fitting trainers squeaking and squelching as he looked for the corridor leading to his "suite."

Observing all from his post of authority, Zeke's suspicious demeanour was now replaced by amusement, which added a dash of character to a face as bland as the grits Thelonious would never eat again, not even if the alternative meant starving to death. He pointedly ignored the clerk as he toddled past, the camera bag on his shoulder banging painfully against his hip as he wheeled his suitcase and stepladder behind him, disappearing into the bowels of the motor lodge.

Thelonious's suite was located near the lift he didn't know existed and across from an alcove with an ice machine and vending machines selling cavity-inducing snacks and cloyingly sweet soft drinks. Zeke was probably pissing himself with laughter for having fobbed off a room nobody else wanted on an unsuspecting guest. Just as Thelonious wondered how much worse things could get, he heard a baby crying. And it sounded very close by.

Freeing the folding stepladder from its bungee cord, he set it up by the door and climbed up to insert the key card. "Open Sesame!" he chuffed, waiting for the little red light to turn green.

The light remained red. The baby's cries got louder.

Thelonious tried again, pushing down on the door handle with such force he thought it would snap off in his paw. He let out an angry roar, which was surpassed in volume by the now-squalling infant. Hitching his camera bag onto his sore shoulder, he dragged his suitcase and its clumsily reattached stepladder back up the corridor and into the frigid lobby. The puddle of rainwater he'd left at reception was still there; with any luck Zeke would slip in it and break his neck. Clambering onto his suitcase, Thelonious slapped the key card down on the counter, nearly upsetting the container of pens.

The clerk's face was buried in a magazine with a glossy cover photo of a man and a boy dressed in camouflage gear. The pair beamed with pride, posing with their rifles and the carcass of a freshly killed deer. Thelonious could almost smell the blood oozing from the page and wished it belonged to the murderous hunters instead of their innocent victim.

"Y'all need somethin'?" mumbled Zeke from behind his hunting porn.

"I can't get into my room."

"Did y'all put the card in the right way? A green light's 'sposed to come on."

"It didn't."

"No green light?"

"No."

"Hmm…"

"The card probably needs re-coding."

"Way-ell, Ah don't know…" Reaching for a pen, Zeke resumed his ear poking. "Should be workin' fine."

"It isn't working at all!" snapped Thelonious, seconds away from ripping the clerk's head off. He might be more advanced in his species, but that didn't mean he couldn't hear the ancestral call.

Snatching up the key card, Zeke disappeared with it into the back office.

As Thelonious teetered on his suitcase awaiting the clerk's return, a rain-drenched young couple with a baby entered the lobby. After some hesitation, they made their way toward reception. The man held what appeared to be a printed reservation; he kept reading and rereading it as if uncertain he'd come to the right place. Setting down the baby carrier, the woman grabbed the paper from his hand, looking it over as well. Upon seeing Thelonious, the infant's face pinched up into an angry red ball, its toothless maw summoning forth a wail capable of bringing down buildings. Grabbing up baby and carrier, the couple glared accusingly at Thelonious.

Zeke finally reappeared, all but throwing the key card at Thelonious. "If it don't work, thare ain't nothin' else Ah kin do."

Shoving the card into his trouser pocket, Thelonious hopped down from the suitcase, rearranged his gear and started back in the direction of the corridor he'd just come from, though not without first treating the couple to an extravagant display of his teeth. The woman's sharp intake of breath kept him chortling all the way to his door, though his amusement quickly ended once he'd entered his "suite." Indeed, the only thing suite-like about it was the musty-looking sofa and coffee table that had been wedged into an extra few feet of living space. The standard motor lodge décor offered no surprises and was as questionably hygienic as Thelonious had come to expect in his travels. The soggy patches he'd left on the carpet were probably the closest it had been to a cleaning since the place was built. Unfortunately, the moisture soaking into the fibres also made the room smell of wet dog.

Pulling back the drapes so he could open a window, Thelonious was greeted by a vista of overflowing rubbish bins. Despite the odour of damp inside, the smell outside was surely worse. He could see a run-down playing field in the near distance and behind it a billboard partially obscured by trees. The words "Risen" and "Jehoshaphat" were visible.

Thelonious stripped off his sodden garments and toddled into the bathroom. One look at the miserly showerhead convinced him to run a bath. A folding card on the bathroom counter asked guests to please be "green" by reusing towels and bedding. Thelonious wasn't fooled. It was all about higher profits and saving on overhead, not saving the environment.

Freshly bathed and in his pyjamas, he phoned out for a pizza, then climbed into bed with the telly remote. A film before bedtime sounded just the ticket. The screen filled with the shiny face of a middle-aged man who looked as if he made a habit of lurking around schoolyards. Waterfalls cascaded down his cherubic cheeks. "Jesus needs you to save the orphans!" he pleaded, his high-pitched voice quaking with sobs. "Heaven awaits those who give!" The camera changed angles, revealing a packed auditorium. Several ushers were sprinting up and down the aisles with plastic buckets. Audience members filled them with envelopes and cash.

The camera returned to the stage, pulling back to reveal a blonde escapee from a doll factory standing reverently behind the speaker, her painted face matching his in its wretchedness. She flung her chubby arms outward as if to embrace the audience. "Praise the Lawd!"

"Hallelujah!" cried the crowd, the camera panning over their ecstatic faces. The man on stage was now weeping uncontrollably along with his plasticised companion. A toll-free phone number appeared at the bottom of the screen, urging viewers to call in with their credit card information.

Thelonious pressed the channel button on the remote. He tried to go higher, then lower, even inputting numbers at random. The preacher refused to budge. Even the OFF button couldn't get rid of him. Clambering down from the bed, he fiddled with the manual controls on the television's front panel. The preacher wasn't going anywhere. In fact, he'd begun to sing a hymn, his cloying voice making Thelonious feel as if he needed another bath. He yanked the plug out of the electrical socket. So much for that film....

After a greasy pepperoni pizza (he'd ordered anchovies), Thelonious was snoring in minutes. Not even the crying baby and the occasional rattle of ice from the ice machine could rouse him. He awakened the next morning to a shard of sunlight coming through a gap in the curtains. Lumbering out of bed, he pulled them open the rest of the way. The world was washed clean by the rain; even the rubbish bins had been emptied.

On duty at reception was Zeke, who looked as if he'd never gone home, his navy-blue lapel having received another snowfall of dandruff in the night. His pink-rimmed eyes were riveted to a mini TV behind the counter, so he didn't bother to glance up when Thelonious returned his key card. Someone on the television was talking about a bank robbery, though Thelonious forgot about it as soon as he stepped outside into the brilliant morning sunshine.

As he drove out of the motor lodge's car park, a patrol car entered at the opposite end, coming to a lurching halt in front of the lobby. Had Thelonious not turned onto the connector road leading to the interstate, he might've seen Zeke hopping up and down in front of a sheriff's deputy and pointing in his direction.

Chapter Two

Manhunt Continues for "Animal Dwarf Bandits" in Bank Robbery!
—Front page headline from the *Pinewood Times-Courier*

NATE JESSOP COULD HARDLY wait to get home to show his folks his article on the front page of their local newspaper. He'd been at it like a hound dog in heat since graduating from his journalism course at the community college. Maybe he'd had to drive thirty-two miles each way in his beat-up red Chevy pickup, but it'd sure been worth it. So had the long hours working at the hardware store in the next town as he earned money to pay for classes and all that gasoline he needed to get to those classes. That old truck ate it like nobody's business, but he couldn't afford anything else. The pickup actually belonged to his pa, though Nate kind of inherited it since Earl Jessop didn't drive now that his driver's license had been suspended for good. Since Nate paid for the insurance, upkeep and registration, the truck was pretty much his when you thought about it.

It'd taken Nate almost four years to finish the two-year college course, though that wasn't because he was some dumb hillbilly. There was only so much money he could make stocking shelves and helping customers over at Joe's Hardware. Old Joe was as nice as could be and a good Christian too. He even gave Nate extra hours when he didn't need to. Nate had been lucky to have the job, considering there wasn't much of anything in these parts when it came to earning money—or earning it legally. Most folks never left here. Instead they stuck around and did nothing or scraped together a living doing odd jobs, though there was only so much landscaping that needed doing or firewood that needed selling.

The lucky ones had their own businesses—like Luke, who had a diner over on Main Street. Pretty much everybody in town hung out at Luke's, since there was nowhere else to hang out unless you wanted to drive a million miles to get there. Sometimes Nate dropped in after school for a cup of Luke's real strong coffee to perk him up for a night of homework. The coffee had another purpose too—it delayed returning home to the disapproving scowl of his pa, who couldn't understand why his son was going to so much trouble to get an education.

"Ah done jus' fine and Ah never got *me* no fancy education!" Earl always said, though his attitude changed some when Nate landed the job at the *Pinewood Times-Courier* and started bringing more money into the household.

His boss Joe had the patience of a saint as he listened to Nate jabbering about his class assignments, including those that required him to sit in on court cases—real honest-to-goodness ones at the county courthouse with folks on trial for theft or drunk driving or even assault. He'd have to write up what happened just like in a genuine newspaper story and hand it in to his teacher for a grade.

Although he knew it wasn't very Christian of him, Nate sometimes wished he had a pa like Joe. He knew his boss was just being polite, but he appreciated getting a timeout from being put down and made to feel like he was nothing all the time. His folks acted like having a goal in life—*aspirations*—was somehow wrong. Okay, his ma wasn't half as bad as his pa, but she was so goldurn scared of her husband she agreed with everything he said, even if he claimed the sky was green and the grass was blue. It was so unfair! Nate had been a good kid. He went to church every Sunday and never got into trouble with drugs or got some girl in trouble either. Heck, he'd barely been out of diapers before he was doing chores around the house and helping Pastor Robinson over at Trinity Baptist. But from the way his pa acted you'd think he'd been some juvenile delinquent crackhead.

Nobody in Nate's town had gone to college. Many hadn't made it through high school. And they sure as heck never got anything *published*—not unless you counted the MINDY-LOU HARRIS SUCKS DICK someone had scrawled inside a toilet stall in the boys' restroom during Nate's senior year. He supposed that technically it *was* a form of journalism since it reported the truth, Nate and his friends being among the boys who'd got their rocks off thanks to Mindy-Lou. But he wanted a better life—and that meant getting out of here before he got some Mindy-Lou pregnant and ended up living with her in a stinky trailer, along with their screaming brats. That'd been the fate of most of his classmates, including those that now had meth labs. No one messed with *those* guys, not even the cops, though that wasn't surprising since they got a piece of the action. If Nate wanted to, he could bust their operation wide open and make a name for himself, not only taking down the local meth trade, but every crooked cop in the county. He often fantasised about the exposé he'd write on small-town police corruption and small-time drug manufacturers and how all the big-city newspapers would come running to his door with job offers. Heck, they'd be fighting over him!

19

But Nate didn't want to end up dead in a field with his nuts stuffed in his mouth—which was exactly what would happen too. Nobody around here *really* wanted to do anything about the meth problem—there was too much money to be made and too many pockets to line. So Nate decided to pursue another story—one that wouldn't bring trouble to his doorstep. He still liked the idea of being a crime reporter, and this recent bank robbery could be his ticket to the big time if he went after it. Maybe he wouldn't set off any fireworks in Atlanta, but there were plenty of smaller cities that would be real glad to have a hardworking young reporter like Nate Jessop on their staff.

As for Nate's folks, they'd be stuck in this mud hole until the day they died. His pa drank like a fish and collected welfare for a disability that only became a problem when there was work to do. As for his ma, she walked around on eggshells, acting like the good church-going lady she was and never putting a foot wrong. Not that this stopped her husband from lashing out with his fist if he thought she'd back-talked him about something. When she wasn't hiding in the house with a black eye or split lip, she'd put in a few hours at Luke's Diner waiting tables during lunchtime. She could always count on a Sunday shift too, since Sundays were real busy with folks coming in to eat lunch after church. Earl Jessop usually gave his fist a rest when a Sunday was approaching—his wife never missed a church service and he didn't want questions being asked. Anyways, he liked the tips she brought home. Folks seemed to be more generous after sitting through one of Pastor Robinson's fire-and-brimstone sermons. Nate suspected Luke felt kind of sorry for his ma, which was why he threw her the occasional bone, work-wise. Not that it changed anything. The money only went toward buying more liquor for his pa.

Nate had a sister just shy of nineteen, while he'd recently turned a worldly twenty-two. Kimmie-Mae lived with her boyfriend Chester in a rusty old trailer in the woods. They already had three kids (one being Chester's from another woman now doing time for using and selling meth). A flea-bitten pit bull never allowed off its chain hung around in their scrappy yard, barking and whining from sun-up to sundown until it eventually fell asleep from exhaustion. Sometimes Nate thought about going over there when nobody was home and rescuing the poor mutt. But if he did that, he'd need to rescue every dog in the county, since this was how most folks treated their animals. The young couple collected their welfare payments and food stamps and Medicaid and anything else they could get for free, with Chester conveniently forgetting to report his income from cutting down trees he had no legal right to cut down, chopping them up, then driving outside the county to sell the unseasoned firewood from out of the back of his truck to customers who'd never see him again. He also sold meth, though only as a favour to friends. Or so he claimed.

Nah, Nate's family would never get out of here. It was too late for them. But it wasn't too late for *him*.

Sitting at his desk inside the double-wide trailer that functioned as the command centre for Pinewood County's only newspaper the *Pinewood Times-Courier*, Nate read his "animal dwarf bandits" article for the third time, his sun-freckled face nearly splitting in half from grinning so much. He was a real reporter now with a real future ahead of him. He wanted to go out and celebrate, except he didn't have anyone to celebrate *with*.

That evening Nate flew into the house as if he had wings on his feet, waving his copy of the newspaper in the air like a flag of victory. His folks were at the supper table eating ham and grits, his pa's meaty fist wrapped possessively around a can of beer. They hadn't even waited for him and he was only ten minutes late! And that was because he'd been talking with his boss, who'd just given him the green light to pursue the bank robbery story. Old man Clemson loved to chew the fat—sometimes it was impossible to get away from him. He was one of those conspiracy theorists, so a five-minute conversation ended up lasting an hour when he got going.

Once again Nate had to hear about how some "New World Order" was behind everything—from deadly diseases to race wars. "The government's takin' away the freedoms of the American people!" insisted Clemson for the millionth time. "We need to git every last one them socialists out of office before they destroy this country completely. Mark my words, Nate, it'll happen unless the American people wake up to what's *really* goin' on!"

Nate's boss sometimes reminded him of his pa, except he wasn't mean as a snake and quick with his fist. Plus old man Clemson could construct an argument to the point where you actually believed it, whereas Earl Jessop—who always managed to sound like a backwoods' hillbilly every time he opened his mouth—was as dumb as a bucket of rocks. Despite the crackpot ideas, Nate liked Mr. Clemson. Anyways, he was only saying what lots of other folks around here said.

As Nate approached the supper table, his pa looked up at him and scowled. His ma stared at her plate, pushing grits around with her fork as if she needed her husband's permission to eat them. A large cross hung on the dining room wall. Its presence made the room feel smaller than it was. Suddenly Nate couldn't breathe. The air was being sucked out of the room and out of his lungs. Though he still clutched it in his hand, he'd forgotten all about the copy of the *Pinewood Times-Courier* with his story in it.

"'Bout goldurn time y'all showed up!" barked Earl Jessop. "This here ain't some fancy restaurant where folks got nothin' better to do but be waitin' on y'all." He poked at a back tooth with a fingernail, plucking out a shred of ham. Returning it to his mouth, he chewed and swallowed it.

"Sorry, Pa. But I had to—"

"So when y'all gittin' a *real* job and supportin' your pa?" interrupted Earl, conveniently forgetting the increased financial contributions to the household Nate been making since he'd started working at the *Times-Courier*. Earl's disapproving grimace showed a landscape of missing teeth, those still remaining stained sewage-brown from a lifetime spent chewing tobacco and avoiding dentists. Nate couldn't remember the last time he'd seen his ma kiss him. Though he couldn't remember the last time his pa had been within spitting distance of a toothbrush either.

"What y'all got in your hand, boy?"

Suddenly Nate remembered the reason for his eagerness to get home. Unfolding the newspaper, he set it carefully on the table alongside his pa's empty plate, making sure his article about the bank robbery was face up. "See? I'm on the front page!"

Earl glanced down at it and snorted. "*Where?* Ah don't see your picture nowhere."

"That's my story!" Nate pointed to the article, which fought for space with news about a church jumble sale and a stolen pickup truck that had been recovered. Aside from the fact that the town where the robbery had taken place wasn't even in Pinewood County, readers of the *Pinewood Times-Courier* preferred good news over bad. He was lucky old man Clemson had run his story at all, especially on the front page.

Nate's ma tried to show a little enthusiasm. "Now Earl, don't be stealin' the boy's thunder. Cain't y'all see how excited he is?" She daintily wiped the corners of her mouth with a cloth napkin, careful not to smear her Avon lipstick. Everybody else used paper napkins, but Nate's ma had standards and liked things to be all proper-like. Not that his pa noticed. He'd already used his to blow his nose in.

"*Excited* don't pay no bills. When's this boy of y'all's gonna realise he's a growed-up man now and needs to start pullin' his weight, not be off gallivantin' for some newspaper like that Superman feller. What's his name ag'in?" Earl slapped the side of his large head as if it might spur some activity inside.

"Y'all mean that Clark Kent feller?" offered his wife. "Oh Lordy, was he ever handsome!"

"That's the one! And y'all watch your mouth, missus— don't be takin' the good Lord's name in vain!" Earl made as if to hit his wife, but evidently thought better of it with his son present. Although Nate had never caught him hitting her (not that his ma would've admitted to it), his pa's fist was connected to a very short fuse. Nate had been on the wrong end of it often enough as a boy to know.

"As for Mr. Nathan big-shot newspaper ree-porter, Ah dunno where y'all been gittin' such highfalutin' ideas into that head of yours, thinkin' y'all better'n the rest of us. We-yall, Ah got me some *real* news to report so listen up good. Y'all ain't better—and it's about time y'all knew it too!" Earl took a swig from his beer can and belched. "Y'all been actin' too big for your britches ever since goin' to that thare community college. Ah knew no good would come of it." He turned to his wife for confirmation. "Didn't Ah say that way back when?"

Nate hated the hot tears burning the backs of his eyelids. But he hated his pa even more.

He'd show him. He'd show him *real* good.

Chapter Three

BOILED PEANUTS.

The shells were stained an ominous dark colour as they soaked in an oily-looking liquid. Before Thelonious could change his mind, the man at the boiled peanut stand had scooped some into a large Styrofoam cup and stuck his palm out for payment. Taking the cup back to the Mini, Thelonious sat at the steering wheel chomping through the softened casings to reach the peanuts, spitting the masticated shells out the window. He gave up halfway through, dumping the remaining peanuts onto the dirt. Noticing that the vendor had stepped away, he quickly lowered himself down from the car, took a few shots of the peanut stand, then went off in search of new subject matter.

Today that subject matter would be barns.

Thelonious photographed working barns and barns so long abandoned they'd turned to rubble. Each had a story, though most told of good fortune gone bad. Where were the farmers who'd kept feed and livestock inside them? If they'd met with financial hardship, surely these properties would've gone to the county or the bank by now. In England land was too valuable to fall into such disuse; a developer would've built cookie-cutter housing estates or turned a neglected barn into luxury flats with luxury price tags. Considering the number of signs offering acreage for sale, land must be cheap and plentiful around here. Thelonious wondered if he should pick up a few acres himself. Maybe he could get a little cabin built to use as a getaway when the English winters became too much.

By late afternoon a tired and hungry Thelonious was ready to pack it in for the day—until he saw the ruined timber barn. It was set well back from the road in a field so long untended it actually seemed to consume the structure. An oak tree had fallen onto the roof, causing it to collapse. The tree was thriving and had even become part of the barn, feeding new life into something left to die. Parking at the edge of what once had been a driveway, Thelonious got out of the Mini. He stood for a moment perusing the site. Slinging his camera bag over one shoulder, he trundled forth into the overgrown field. A NO TRESPASSING sign lay on the ground, covered over with weedy detritus. It was still attached to a chain that had fallen down between two rotted posts. He passed right by, never seeing it.

Thelonious photographed the barn from various angles, changing lenses as he saw fit. Although the weight of his camera bag was a nuisance, he dared not set it down for fear it would be swallowed by the overgrowth. Approaching the barn's entrance, he noticed several bales of hay inside that had been left there to rot. Rust-covered farm implements lay scattered about both inside and out. He included them in some of the images, since they lent extra character to the scene. He even captured a triangle of sunlight coming through the barn's collapsed roof as it returned the mouldering hay to its original golden splendour, zooming in when a mouse poked its head out to feel the sunshine on its whiskers. The light shifted and changed hue, adding shadow, depth and richness to his compositions. Had Thelonious's attention not been caught by a ramshackle assemblage of containers off to one side, he might've seen the figure skulking in the shadows behind him.

A rusty metal cylinder with a triangular-shaped lid had been set up in a corner of the barn. An encrusted pipe had been attached to the top, the elbow joint bending it sideways connecting it to a worm-eaten wooden barrel; its remaining iron bands had turned green with corrosion. Glass jugs and jam jars lay strewn about on the dirt floor. Some looked as if they had mouse droppings on them. Thelonious's nostrils detected the odour of fermenting grains. It appeared that he'd stumbled upon a moonshine still.

As Thelonious framed it in his viewfinder, he heard a loud explosion. A bullet whistled past his right ear, nearly taking his deerstalker hat with it.

"Hold it right thare!"

A wiry old man with a shotgun stepped out from the shadows. He planted himself solidly behind Thelonious. A long scraggly beard hung from his chin; it would've been white if not for the dribbles of tobacco juice. Thelonious was pretty sure he saw things moving in it.

The ancient codger aimed the firearm at Thelonious's chest, the brown sticks of his arms surprisingly steady as they stuck out from his tattered bib overalls. "This here's private property!" he shouted.

Thelonious took a few steps back, feeling his bowels loosening. "I thought the barn was abandoned?" he croaked.

"*Abandoned?*" The old man spat into the dirt. "This here barn ain't abandoned!"

"I must've made a mistake."

"Ah'll say y'all made a mistake! This here's my farm!"

"Sorry."

"Hmmph…" The farmer squinted hard at his intruder, his creased face like a dried plum above the beard.

Thelonious shifted the camera bag to his other shoulder. "I'll just be on my way then."

But the farmer had other ideas. He moved nearer, closing the gap between them. "Did that no 'count Bobby Ray Tuggle send y'all down here to steal my corn liquor?"

"No!" Thelonious shook his head until he thought it would fall off. The cosy relationship between the old man's index finger and the shotgun's trigger was making him nervous.

"Y'all don't know Bobby Ray?"

"I don't know *anyone*!"

"Okay. If'n y'all say so."

Hoping this was the end of it, Thelonious turned to go.

"Not so dang fast! Didn't y'all see my 'no trespassing' sign?"

"*What* 'no trespassing' sign?"

"Y'all walked right on past it. It's thare, plain as day!" A skeletal brown finger pointed toward the barn's gaping entrance. "C'aint miss it!"

"But I didn't see any sign!"

"Ah shoot trespassers." The farmer gave Thelonious a grisly brown grin. "Shot me one last year. He's buried out back of the barn. Wanna see?"

"No!"

"Trespassin's illegal in these parts."

"But it was a mistake!"

"Y'all breakin' the law!"

"But—"

The old man relocated his aim from Thelonious's chest to his head. "Now git off my land, ya thievin' varmint!"—he hollered—"'afore Ah make y'all into a stew for my supper!"

Although Thelonious had no desire to become the special of the day at Chez Hillbilly, he found his exit blocked by the gun-toting pensioner, who didn't appear particularly inclined to let him by. Another bullet whizzed past, this time singeing the fur on his ear. The farmer's maniacal cackling echoed in the dilapidated barn. "Ah ain't never had me no baar stew before!"

Thelonious backed away until he could go no farther; he'd bumped up against a wall. Skirting it, he tried to get around the old man, who looked as if he were about to take another shot. Suddenly Thelonious noticed a door hanging half off its hinges. He hadn't seen it until now because his view had been blocked by the bales of hay. To reach it he'd need to cross to the other side of the barn, which would put him directly in front of the farmer. Fortunately, the old nutter seemed to be expecting him to leave the same way he'd come in and had turned to face in that direction. Thelonious had also begun to suspect that the farmer's eyesight wasn't too good, especially with the thickening shadows. The sun no longer shone through the barn's buckled roof. Any lingering daylight was concealed by the oak tree that had fallen through.

Clutching his camera bag to his chest, Thelonious took off in a lumbering run, his short legs propelling him toward the lopsided door. He barrelled through it, the splintering wood sounding like another shotgun blast as the door broke away from its frame. A real blast followed, poking a jagged hole into the wall near where the door had been.

Thelonious's ill-fitting trainers crunched through the weedy field in the direction of the road. The Union Jack on the Mini's roof gave off one final blaze of colour before fading into the dusk. Tossing his camera gear inside, he levered himself up onto the driver's seat, his claws nearly ripping the upholstery when he pulled shut the door. As he started the engine, a bullet dinged off the bonnet like a stone skipping over the surface of a pond.

The little car rocketed into the road, its rear tyres kicking up a chaos of dust and gravel. When he turned to look behind him, Thelonious saw the trigger-happy old farmer standing in the road ready to take another shot.

Chapter Four

EVERY NIGHT AFTER SUPPER Nate would sit on the sofa with his ma watching TV. It was his small way of giving her moral support. The Jessops probably looked like millions of other American families, with Nate's pa relaxing on the recliner with a beer and his ma fiddling with a piece of needlepoint she'd only end up donating to the church jumble sale. All that was missing was a dog. They did have one a few years ago, but it'd run off and never come back. Nate often wished he'd done the same.

The Jessops still had an old-fashioned television set with a picture tube that stuck out in back like a fat lady's behind. They didn't have the flat-screen high-definition kind that made everything look so real you could almost reach through the screen and touch it all. Nate's pa refused to let the family buy one even though they could've afforded some of the smaller models selling at the Walmart a few towns away. Earl

Jessop claimed they were the Devil's invention. "If'n the good Lord wanted us to look at false images tryin' to fool us into believin' they's real, he wouldn't have given us nature to enjoy!" he preached, waving his beer can in the air to highlight his point.

Nate had nothing against enjoying nature, though he couldn't remember the last time his pa had, especially when chores were involved. That responsibility always fell to Nate and his ma. On weekends Nate would usually be outside hammering away at something that needed hammering while his ma was on her bony knees pulling out weeds by hand when she wasn't working a shift at Luke's Diner. The yard had more weeds than grass—and what grass there was had pretty much up and died. Luke said they needed to re-sod and that his landscaper brother could do the job at a discount. But Earl wouldn't hear of it.

"Ah ain't havin' that good-for-nothin' brother of that good-for-nothin' Lucas Jenner pokin' his nose in my private business. Next thing he'll be wantin' to put in rosebushes and statues of nekkid folks! Why, we got all the landscapin' we need!" he cried, pointing a thick finger in the direction of the faded American flag that drooped from a pole on the family's front porch. "God bless America!"

Nate couldn't imagine anything as pretty as roses growing at their house. Nothing could grow at their house. Nothing but weeds.

A wooden cross the twin of the one in the dining room hung on the wall above Nate and his mother's heads like a constant reminder of their sins. He felt it burning a hole into his neck and rubbed the skin as if he could cool it down some.

"S'matter, boy? Y'all got fleas?" Earl chortled. Suddenly his eyes turned mean. "Told y'all not to go messin' around with that thare Weaver girl. Them Weavers ain't nothin' but trouble. White trash, that's all they is."

"But I ain't been messin' around with that Weaver girl!" Nate winced as soon as the words left his mouth. He hated falling into what he'd come to think of as "Hillbilly Talk," but his pa seemed to bring it out of him like a nasty rash. He'd better watch his step if he hoped to get out of this hick town because Nate was willing to bet none of those newspaper reporters at the *Atlanta Journal-Constitution* spoke like they lived in a backwoods' trailer. Bad enough his kid sister lived in one with that meth-dealing boyfriend of hers. Not that Nate planned to go broadcasting it to people he needed to impress.

"Them Weavers don't even go to our church," continued Earl, getting more riled up by the minute. "They ain't nothin' but heathens! Lucifer'll be real busy when them no-good Weavers arrive on Hell's doorstep!" He took a noisy slurp from his beer and burped. "Ya'll steer clear of that white trash Weaver girl, hear?"

"Yes, Pa."

Satisfied he'd done a good job of parenting, Earl slouched lower in his beat-up vinyl recliner and scratched his crotch. Nate could still remember when the family had bought that recliner—he'd been a little kid, with Kimmie-Mae barely out of diapers. It'd been a real big event too. Nate and his sister had been strapped into their child's seats in the back, his ma sitting up front with his pa, who drove them all the way to Valdosta to visit Sears. Nate's ma had got all dressed up for the occasion. She was hoping for a new washing machine, but that didn't happen. Instead his pa picked out a fancy recliner with a special switch that raised your feet up and moved you forward and backward. Now the thing looked like something you'd find at the dump. Afterward they'd gone to Dairy Queen as a treat, getting burgers *and* ice cream. Nate's ma didn't say a word on the drive home. She just sniffed and kept dabbing at her eyes with a tissue.

Earl turned his attention back to the cop show he'd been watching, the TV screen framed by his oddly shaped feet. His once-white socks were stained yellow from sweat and the powder he used to control foot odour. The stuff did nothing to solve the problem. The room reeked every time he took off his shoes. Nate wished he'd keep them on or at least wear slippers, but it was like his pa enjoyed forcing everyone to breathe in his stinky-feet fumes. He wondered how his ma could stand it, especially since the couple still slept in the same room and shared the same bed. Maybe all those years of marriage had burned her sense of smell out of her nostrils.

The local news came on. Or at least it was local if you considered a city almost one-hundred-fifty miles away "local." The anchor-man was introducing a story about a bank robbery that had happened earlier that afternoon. It had been committed by the armed bandits wearing animal masks. The anchor kept referring to them as "dwarves." Nate wasn't exactly sure if the term was politically correct, but in his neck of the woods "politically correct" usually meant guns, Jesus and the Republican Party. The bank robbery had taken place only a few miles away from Nate's town—and this time there'd been a shooting.

The anchor-man was replaced by a pretty blonde female reporter standing outside a branch of Great Southern Savings and Loan. People could be seen milling around in the background, most of them sheriff's deputies. The reporter spoke with high-octane excitement into a hand-held microphone, blinking rapidly at the camera as if she had a lash caught in her eye. Apparently the bank manager had been shot in the foot by one of the robbers, whom eyewitnesses claimed used an old-fashioned gun like gangsters had back in the old days. "He's expected to pull through," said the reporter, actually grinning when she added that the shooter had worn a goat mask.

"World's goin' to hell in a handbasket!" Nate's pa slammed his beer can down on the end table, avoiding the coaster placed there by his wife. "This here's what comes of not welcomin' the Lord into your life!" Earl snorted with disdain. "Y'all ask me, it's them pot-smokin', queer-lovin' Democrats behind it. Mark my words—they ain't gonna be watchin' out for us regular folks when all them Niggras and Muslims come to steal what's ours! Ah said it before and

Ah'll say it ag'in—we gotta start preparin' *now* before things start to git *real* bloody! We gotta stock up on guns, ammo, food…"

Nate had heard his pa's End of the World sermon so many times he could recite it in his sleep. It was the same sermon most folks in these parts gave every time something bad happened. A terrorist attack on the opposite side of the world, an increase in the price of a gallon of gas, a homosexual elected to public office—the end of civilisation was coming! Nate wondered how his pa planned to fight off so many enemies single-handedly when he wouldn't even get up out of his stinky recliner except to use the toilet.

"Please Pa, I need to hear this. This is the story I'm working on for the—"

The recliner groaned menacingly as Earl made to get up. "Y'all tryin' to shush me, boy?"

A clammy sweat began to seep from Nate's pores. Although he knew he could take on his pa if he had to what with youth on his side, he knew his ma would be the one to suffer for it. Earl Jessop might've retired his belt and his fist when it came to giving his son a good hiding, but he hadn't retired them when it came to his wife, though never in front of witnesses. Earl didn't like gossip, especially if that gossip included *him*. The local church ladies loved to run off at the mouth, so Mrs. Jessop hid her bruises out of shame, blaming herself for her failings as a wife.

"But Earl, it's for the boy's work!" she pleaded, her voice holding about as much authority as a mouse's.

"*Work?*" thundered Earl, itching for a fight. "Y'all mean that big-city newspaper he drives to every day in *my* truck? What's he do over thare—make coffee? That boy of y'alls gotta learn some *ree*-spect!"

Nate's ma flattened herself against the back of the sofa as if she could disappear into the dusty cushions. It was rare for her to stand up to her husband. Rare and dangerous.

Earl finally settled down, his hankering for a fight replaced by his need to finish his beer. "Hmmph…" was his last word on the subject.

Nate listened to the rest of the news report, making mental notes on potential subjects he could interview. The shooter had fled the scene with his fellow robbers, all of whom were seen getting into a car driven by a chicken, though the reporter coyly assured viewers it was more likely someone wearing a chicken mask. While one eyewitness claimed the getaway car was a white Ford sedan, another said it was a red Chevy hatchback, with still another insisting it was a small foreign car that might've been blue.

Or purple.

Nate felt like someone had just set fire to his nuts. Those "animal dwarf bandits" were right here on his doorstep. This story could be his ticket to the big time!

Chapter Five

"Animal Dwarf Bandits" Strike Again! Bank Manager Shot!
—Front page headline from the *Johnstown Herald*

THELONIOUS ROLLED OVER on the hard mattress of his motel-issue bed and groaned. Every swallow of saliva was a torturous scrape of sandpaper against the back of his throat. Rivers dripped from his nostrils. Even his muscles ached. Sneezing his way into the bathroom, he clambered up onto the desk chair he'd left by the vanity. The furry face staring back at him from the mirror didn't belong to his usual handsome self. His eyes were bloodshot, his muzzle damp and crusty. He wouldn't be winning any prizes for his good looks today.

Between his near-fatal encounter with psycho Elmer Fudd and getting caught in a downpour, no wonder he was under the weather. A few tablets and he'd be right as rain. But when Thelonious phoned the front desk to find out if there was a GP's surgery in the area, he needed to repeat himself so many times he would've been better off drawing a picture of a stethoscope and delivering it in person.

"*Surgery?*" repeated the clerk. "If'n y'all need surgery, call nine-one-one!"

"I don't need surgery!" croaked Thelonious. "I need a *GP's* surgery!"

"A *what?*"

"A doctor. I need to see a doctor!"

"Why'nt y'all say so in the first place?"

"I thought I did."

"We-yall, Ah cain't afford to go to no fancy doctors." The clerk's tone indicated he considered Thelonious part of some privileged elite. "Look in the phone book!"

Thelonious found one in the nightstand tucked beneath a Gideon Bible. Only a handful of doctors were listed, but he saw plenty of funeral directors should his illness become more serious. A general practitioner was located in the same town as his motel. They squeezed him in as an emergency, though Thelonious had to exaggerate his symptoms before the receptionist finally granted him an appointment.

The doctor's office was located in what the woman had described as a "strip mall," which turned out to be an unappealing yet functional structure housing a collection of shops and businesses along with a car park. Thelonious found Dr. Bardeen's practice sandwiched between a dollar store and a Chinese restaurant/takeaway that had a pair of feral cats loitering outside the glass-fronted door. No doubt they'd been attracted by the smell of fish wafting out. He hoped they didn't end up on the menu.

Upon arrival, Thelonious was presented with a clipboard holding a sheaf of paperwork he was told to fill out. He was also asked to provide his insurance card. When he explained that he didn't have one, he received a disapproving scowl. "Y'all don't have insurance?" drawled the receptionist. She glared down at him from her cubicle window as if he'd come to rob her. "Then y'all need to pay *now*. Credit or debit card— we don't take personal cheques. We also need your driver's licence."

Thelonious wanted to ask why, since he hadn't planned to drive the doctor to lunch. Instead he removed his UK credit card and his UK driving licence from his wallet, holding them high above his head so the receptionist could reach them more easily. He heard a swivel chair banging into a metal filing cabinet as she stood up and leaned out the cubicle window to grab them from his paw, clearly annoyed by the inconvenience this new patient was causing her.

"What's *this*?" A talon the shade of a rotting strawberry tapped the object in question.

"My driving licence," Thelonious replied in a scratchy growl. Suddenly he heard a high-pitched giggle in the waiting room behind him, followed by a shushing.

"But this here ain't American!" the woman protested. "Ah gotta check with Dr. Bardeen about *this*!"

As he waited for her return, Thelonious felt curious eyes boring into his back. The childish giggling had been joined by adult whispers. Finally the receptionist reappeared. His driving licence and credit card were now accompanied by a receipt he needed to sign. These items had been attached to the clipboard, which she'd almost dropped onto his head when she handed it back down to him. Thelonious couldn't believe it. A charge of $200 and he hadn't even seen the doctor yet!

He looked around for a place to sit, but the only seat low enough to reach without making a spectacle of himself was a plastic child's chair located in a children's play area. A little girl with tangled blonde hair and a finger up one nostril sat in the neighbouring version. She watched Thelonious as if waiting for him to perform like a circus animal. A woman he took to be the mother stared blankly at a television mounted on the wall. The screen showed a young woman waxing ecstatic over a dishwashing liquid.

The other denizens of Dr. Bardeen's waiting room included a dangerously obese woman accompanied by two runny-nosed tots destined to compete with her in the size department. The trio took up the entire length of an imitation-leather sofa, which could've accommodated four adults quite comfortably. They too, seemed to be engrossed in the saga of the washing-up liquid, its happy user having left the kitchen to prance through a colour-enhanced lemon orchard. A man in a greasy Budweiser cap and dirty jeans slouched in an adjacent chair. He picked at his cuticles, flicking bits of dead skin onto the floor in between checking the fare on TV, which had now moved on to a bony-faced brunette shoving a microphone into the faces of excited young women in the studio audience.

Everyone's attention shifted to Thelonious as he claimed the one remaining adult chair, having dragged over the child's version to use as a step. As he reached for a fly-fishing magazine on the end table beside him, he noticed a Bible in amongst the magazines. Was this Dr. Bardeen so incompetent his patients needed to pray before seeing him?

Suddenly the door by the receptionist's station opened. A matronly woman dressed in hot-pink surgical scrubs stepped out. "Mr. Beer?" Her eyes scanned the waiting room. Thelonious assumed Mr. Beer was the man busy butchering his cuticles, but when he failed to respond, the woman repeated the name, this time much louder. When there was still no reply, she glanced at the folder in her hand. "*Thelonious?*"

Acknowledging her with an embarrassed wave of his paw, Thelonious clambered down from his chair, ignoring the wet sniggers coming from the sofa. He hadn't expected to be seen this quickly, especially since the other patients had been waiting longer. Maybe he'd been bumped up the queue?

"Ah'm Miss Sally," Pink-scrubs introduced. "Please follow me, Mr. Beer!" She escorted Thelonious down a corridor with a linoleum floor smudged with dusty orange shoe prints.

"Actually, it's *Bear*," said Thelonious.

"Pardon?"

"My surname's 'Bear,' not 'Beer.'"

"Oh my lord, Ah'm so sorry, Mr. Bear! Miss Pauline must've wrote it down wrong on your chart."

If Miss Pauline was the practice's surly receptionist, Thelonious wasn't surprised she'd got it wrong. She'd probably done it on purpose.

"That's a mighty interestin' name y'all got, considerin'..." Miss Sally stopped without warning, causing Thelonious to collide with her pink-upholstered backside. "Ah never met a *Thee-lonious* before either!"

Rather than going into the story about how he'd been named after jazz great Thelonious Monk, Thelonious merely nodded. The likelihood that anyone from around here had heard of Monk, let alone listened to jazz, seemed pretty remote.

"Y'all mind steppin' up here, Mr. Bear?" Miss Sally indicated the weight scale that had been the reason for the unexpected stop. Thelonious hopped up onto it, waiting while she fiddled with the contraption at the top, writing the result in his chart. She next checked his height, not pushing the issue when he didn't remove his hat. From here they entered a small room furnished with an examination table, two chairs and a long counter with drawers beneath it. A blood-pressure cuff hung from a hook on the wall. Thelonious hoped she wouldn't ask him to get up onto the examination table because she might as well ask him to climb Big Ben.

"Ah just need to check your pressure, so if y'all would set yourself down right here?" Miss Sally patted the seat cushion on one of the chairs, smiling indulgently as Thelonious clambered up onto it, having made use of the step from the examination table. Feeling a sneeze coming on, he clamped his paw over his muzzle. "Bless you!" cried Miss Sally. Reaching for a box of tissues on the counter, she held it toward him. Thelonious grabbed several, swiping them over his wet snout.

"Dr. Bardeen'll be right on in!" Miss Sally vanished in a blur of pink, closing the door softly behind her.

Thelonious waited.

And waited.

The windowless examination room began to feel like a jail cell. If Thelonious had to read the heart-healthy poster tacked to the back of the door one more time he'd be qualified to teach a course on the subject. He wondered if everyone had gone to lunch, forgetting he was still back here. Maybe they were next door at the Chinese place enjoying today's special, Egg Foo Cat. The fluorescent light above his head buzzed relentlessly, giving him a headache. Thelonious shut his eyes and counted to one-hundred, then counted backward. Just as he was about to go into the corridor to find out why he hadn't been seen yet, the door opened. "About bloody time," he muttered when he saw the white lab coat.

After a garbled introduction, Dr. Bardeen told Thelonious to get onto the examination table, watching with ill-humour as his new patient struggled to reach the top, his expression darkening when Thelonious used the cushion of the chair he'd been sitting on as a stepladder. "Exactly what seems to be the trouble?"

With a throaty rumble, Thelonious outlined his symptoms, adding that he'd been perfectly fine until he'd got caught in a thunderstorm. "Do you think it might be pneumonia?" he asked worriedly, unsettled by the fact that Dr. Bardeen had yet to make any notes in his chart. He hadn't even glanced at it. The doctor's expression didn't waver, which increased Thelonious's unease. Everyone knew that doctors went deadpan when delivering bad news. Perhaps things were worse than he thought.

"I'm afraid you've had a wasted trip, Mr. Beer. I don't treat patients of your…um….*species*. I suggest you see a vet."

"A *what?*" Thelonious held his furry chin high. Even Britain's National Health Service had never treated him like this! Granted, he did change GPs more than most patients, but that was only because he hadn't warmed to anyone.

"There's a vet right here in town," continued the doctor, apparently unconcerned that he'd caused offence. "I take my two German Shepherds there. Southern Hospitality Animal Hospital. You'll find them at the other end of Main Street near Luke's Diner." With a cursory nod, he turned to leave. "If they can't help, you can always try a zoo."

Thelonious longed to clamp his teeth onto the doctor's leg until he reached the bone, but he didn't want the arrogant quack calling out animal control. If all he'd needed was to get his blood pressure checked, he could've gone into any American drug store and used their blood-pressure machine for free. He believed he was entitled to a refund. After all, he'd paid for a service that hadn't been rendered. Unfortunately, the smug-faced receptionist didn't share his opinion. Since Thelonious had already seen the doctor and taken up the doctor's time, the fee was binding.

"Ah don't know how y'all do things over thare in England, but this here's the Yew-nited States of America. Y'all cain't git everything for free just 'cause y'all don't wanna pay for it!" She slammed her little window shut, terminating the discussion.

Thelonious stomped out of the office. He had a vet to see.

Returning to the Mini, he noticed that the two feral cats that had been prowling around outside the Chinese restaurant/takeaway were now gone. Inside the place was packed with diners either eating lunch or waiting in a queue to take their lunch with them. One of these diners was Dr. Bardeen, who was seated at the dirty window spooning something into his mouth. Thelonious shook his paw at him as he drove past, throwing in a growl for good measure.

A horse trailer took up several spaces in Southern Hospitality Animal Hospital's crowded car park. Thelonious had no choice but to park behind it. A russet rump mooned him as he levered himself down from the driver's seat, a grassy-smelling fart wafting in his direction. The massive beasts frightened the life out of him. There was something sneaky about them, as if they'd chuck their riders off a cliff if they thought they could get away with it. Thelonious dreaded going inside the building for fear of what else he'd find. This was farming country. For all he knew, the waiting area might be filled with cows, pigs and chickens!

The receptionist turned out to be a pleasant young woman the exact opposite of the sour-faced tyrant at Dr. Bardeen's office. Although taken aback by Thelonious's request to see the doctor, her smile didn't waver. She'd even got his name right, spelling it back to him to make sure. Other than the gassy brute in the car park, there wasn't another horse in sight.

The crowded waiting area smelled of urine and fear along with an underlying scent of pine cleaner. Thelonious claimed the last chair, preferring it to the one with the depressed-looking pit bull terrier cowering beneath it. Tugging his deerstalker hat lower over his ears, he ignored the curious looks from pet owners and several of the animals. The room contained a motley assortment of dogs and cats, some whining and hissing in pet carriers, some attached to leads. The larger canines and many of the smaller ones pulled at their leads as they tried to coax their owners toward the door. Thelonious couldn't blame them. He didn't want to be here either.

Thelonious leafed through a pet-owner's magazine, his trainer-clad feet dangling like bait beneath his chair and attracting the attention of the dog nearest to him—a black mastiff with a bad case of mange. As he attempted to immerse himself in an article about heartworm, the dog shimmied closer, its eyes fixed on his trainers, which Thelonious was unconsciously swinging to and fro. Suddenly the animal pounced. Fastening its lower half to Thelonious's right leg, it began to hump away, oblivious to the presence of its owner, who was humming along with "What a Friend We Have in Jesus" leaking from the ear buds of his iPod.

All eyes turned to Thelonious as he fought to reclaim his

leg. He was certain an old tabby in a pet carrier was laughing at him—he could see its pointy feline teeth gleaming with sadistic glee as he tried everything short of kicking the mangy mutt in the chops. He even dispatched one of his best ursine growls, hoping it might dissuade the creature from its pursuits. Eventually the mastiff's owner took notice.

"Homer! Y'all stop that right now!" he scolded, swatting the dog on its backside before resuming his humming. But Homer had his heart set on achieving a satisfying outcome with Thelonious's leg and couldn't be dissuaded.

Thelonious hadn't met with such single-minded canine determination since Lord Nelson, The Drowned Duck's resident dachshund whose flatulence was as infamous as his ardour. The smell of boiling cabbage would always remind Thelonious of that Norfolk village pub.

Sliding down from his chair, he hobbled toward the receptionist's desk, dragging Homer with him. "Excuse me!" he called.

Stopping her work, the receptionist looked up, clearly puzzled by the interruption. With a shrug, she went back to what she was doing, pausing briefly to answer the phone.

"Hello?" Thelonious waved his paws in the air. "Can you help me?"

"Oh!" The young woman leaned over the desk. "Ah didn't see y'all down thare!"

"I'm in a bit of a bother here." Thelonious indicated the dog. "Will I need to wait much longer?"

The receptionist grinned. "Ah see y'all have met Homer! He likes to do that. Though he ain't gonna be doin' it much after today," she added with a wink.

Coming out from behind the desk, she grabbed Homer's mangy backside and pulled him off Thelonious's molested leg. "Henry!" she called, struggling to keep hold of the dog. "Y'all need to take Homer outside till it's time to see the doc. He's pesterin' folks ag'in!"

Homer's owner heaved himself out of his chair and plodded over. With a spiteful glare at Thelonious, he hooked his fingers into the dog's collar and dragged him out the door.

"They'll probably go on home like last time," the receptionist told Thelonious. "Homer's been in three times already, but Henry keeps changin' his mind. Y'all'd think Henry was the one gittin' fixed instead of Homer!"

Just as Thelonious was about to return to his seat, a pimply-faced lad came to escort him into a smelly examination room where another lad was mopping up a pool of urine. A grey-haired man wearing a dingy white lab coat over what the Yanks called "chinos" entered the room. He clapped Thelonious on the shoulder as if they were old mates. "So how can we help you, Mr. Bear?"

Once again Thelonious provided a summary of his systems, too humiliated to mention his visit with Dr. Bardeen. "I probably just need some tablets," he added helpfully.

"You mean you're not here for your pet?"

Thelonious shook his head.

"Never had one of *your* kind here before," said the veterinarian. "But I'm sure we can fix what ails ya!"

"I hope so."

"You new in town? I haven't seen you around."

"Just passing through."

"That explains it then. In a small town everybody knows everybody—and I'm sure I'd remember *you*! So what's that middle initial of yours stand for? Timothy? Tyler? Thomas? My brother-in-law's named Thomas. He sells insurance. I bet you went right past his office on the way here!"

"It stands for 'Teddy.'" Thelonious wished the man would get on with it already instead of trying to drum up business for his family members.

"*Teddy?* You don't say!" The vet chuckled. "That makes sense…in a way. Grady, give us a hand here?" The request was directed toward the pimply lad, who'd been hovering in the doorway, picking at his spots.

Having been summoned to duty, Grady thrust his hands into Thelonious's armpits, lifting him high in the air and plonking him down on the cold steel examination table as if he were a sack of spuds. Thelonious reached up to straighten his hat, baring his teeth at the careless assistant who'd knocked it askew.

With his thumb the vet gently pulled downward on the flesh beneath Thelonious's eyes, staring into them. "Tell me again how you're feeling. Any pain, body aches, sore muscles?"

Thelonious re-recited his list of symptoms, punctuating them with a hearty sneeze. Grady swiped at his muzzle with a scratchy tissue, then took it upon himself to unbutton Thelonious's shirtfront. Before Thelonious could object, the vet was pressing a stethoscope against his furry chest, nodding thoughtfully as he went along. "There's definitely some congestion. Could turn into bronchitis if you're not careful." He let out a hearty laugh. "If bears can get bronchitis, that is!"

As the vet went to fetch something from a cupboard, Grady stepped forward and began to do up the buttons on Thelonious's shirtfront. Thelonious slapped his hands away, preferring to do the task himself despite the challenges posed by buttons and claws.

"It's just a minor chest infection." The veterinarian pressed a plastic bottle containing some capsules into Thelonious's paw. "Take one in the morning and one at night. If you're no better in a week, come back and see us!"

Another clap on the shoulder sent Thelonious on his way. He'd barely left the room before he heard the vet saying to his assistant: "A bear.... Now *there's* something to tell 'em at the next A.V.M.A. convention!"

When Thelonious returned to the waiting area, he saw that Homer had returned, though this time the mangy Casanova had found someone else's leg to seduce. The receptionist presented Thelonious with a bill for $150. "That includes your meds," she said, making it sound as though he'd snagged a bargain. Between the quack down the road and this horse doctor, it had cost him $350 to be diagnosed and treated for a simple cold!

The next morning Thelonious felt almost like his old self again. A quick strip-wash in his motel bathroom followed by a splash of cologne and he was on his way. He hadn't even driven ten minutes before he encountered another bloodied HE IS RISEN! billboard. Pastor Jehoshaphat Jones seemed like an old friend already. Which reminded him, the revival meeting was a few days away. Since they probably had strict rules against taking photos, Thelonious decided to use his little "covert" camera that resembled a key fob. If he only submitted images in which participants couldn't be identified, he'd be fine as far as his publisher's legal department was concerned. Besides, he had no inclination to chase after people at a religious event to get them to sign release forms.

Thelonious saw a white trailer coming up on his left. Since arriving in the South he'd seen plenty of trailers, the majority of them corroded rust buckets with air conditioning units sticking haphazardly out of their windows. This one was different. Aside from being in excellent nick, it had a giant white cross set onto its roof. A sign out front confirmed that the trailer was a Baptist church. It also contained the following message:

JESUS
DYING TO KNOW YOU

Wanting a closer look, Thelonious executed a careful U-turn, borrowing a portion of a dirt driveway belonging to a farm so he wouldn't obstruct the road. He parked the Mini on the grassy shoulder and got out.

The little church was lovingly maintained. Its white vinyl siding looked recently pressure-cleaned, as did the pavement of the empty parking area and driveway. There wasn't a drop of motor oil anywhere or even a dusting of red Georgia clay. Flowerbeds graced the church's entrance, which was a standard front door typically found on a mobile home. Thelonious could see that great pride had gone into the place—and it was this pride he hoped to capture with his camera.

Thelonious started off with a few deep angle shots, playing tag with the sunlight as it created a dramatic panorama of light and shadow over the trailer's pristine siding. He moved on to progressively broader vistas featuring lots of blue sky behind the white cross on the roof. As he dropped into a deep squat to frame an award-winning shot in the camera's viewfinder, a sheriff's patrol car careened into the driveway. It came to a lurching halt by Thelonious's outthrust backside as the shutter clicked on what would be his final photograph of the day.

The large square head at the steering wheel turned toward Thelonious, who'd lost his balance, landing hard on his bum. The camera flew out of his paws into the grass. "Y'all stop right thare!" shouted the head's owner.

The patrol car listed to one side as a uniformed figure unfolded his bulk from the driver's seat. Slapping a wide-brimmed hat over a military buzz cut, the man stared down at Thelonious. A gun the size of a cannon was cinched to his side along with a Taser and other weapons of torture and coercion. "Y'all made a illegal turn back thare!" The words were barked through a wad of chewing tobacco. A fat thumb gestured toward where Thelonious had performed his careful turnaround.

Brushing off the seat of his trousers, Thelonious drew himself up to his full height, which was sadly lacking unless he was facing off a toddler. The man towered over him like King Kong, his sunglasses mirroring Thelonious's anxious visage back to him. Suddenly he whipped them off, glaring at Thelonious as if he'd just caught a rattlesnake in his chicken coop. The ham hocks of his fists curled and uncurled, ready to wrap themselves around someone's neck; Thelonious hoped it wouldn't be his.

"That thare vee-hicle yours?" The glare took in the Mini Cooper.

"Is there a problem, Officer?"

"It's *Sheriff*." The man spat out a stream of brown juice that landed too near Thelonious's trainers. "Sheriff Grizzle. And Ah asked y'all about that thare vee-hicle."

Thelonious's gut went into a clench-lock. "Yes, it's mine."

"Then Ah take it y'all's got a driver's licence and vee-hicle registration?"

Was Thelonious about to be railroaded into paying some bogus traffic fine? He'd heard about these corrupt Southern cops scamming money from drivers who'd rather pay a bribe than get penalty points on their driving record. As he reached toward his trouser pocket for his wallet, wondering what he should take out first—his licence or a fifty-dollar bill, the sheriff's posture stiffened, his meaty right hand hovering over the butt of his gun. "Easy thare, son! Y'all take it nice and slow now, hear?"

With a trembling paw, Thelonious pulled out his wallet. He was just about to hand over his driving licence when Sheriff Grizzle strode off toward the Mini. "Y'all ain't from around here, Ah take it?" he called over his shoulder, circling the car and peering in through the windows. "Confederate flag, eh?" He rapped his thick knuckles against the Union Jack on the Mini's roof. "Ain't seen too many bears, 'specially thems that kin drive. Ah always thought most of y'all live in the woods like that Yogi Bear feller!" The sheriff let out a liquidy chortle. "Thems that ain't livin' in a zoo, that is. Y'all know Yogi Bear?"

"Not personally, no."

"Ain't been to the zoo in years," continued the sheriff. "Good zoo in Atlanta. Though Ah cain't say the same for the traffic up thare. Rudest goldurn drivers Ah ever done seen! Y'all been to Hotlanta?"

Assuming this must be a nickname for the city, Thelonious shook his head.

Grizzle snorted. "Don't bother goin'."

Having completed his inspection of the Mini Cooper, the sheriff headed back to his vehicle, where he removed his hat, tossing it inside. He stood there watching Thelonious and scratching at the bristles on his head, inadvertently awakening a few flakes of dead skin. Finally he seemed to come to a decision. "Okay, seein' as y'all ain't from around here and Ah'm late gittin' back to the station, Ah'm gonna let it go. *This time*. But next time y'all know better about executin' any of them illegal *yew*-turns." As he stuffed himself back behind the steering wheel, he shook his index finger at Thelonious in warning. "'Cause Ah'll be watchin'!"

The patrol car sped out of the driveway, its tyres leaving twin trails of black rubber on the once-pristine pavement and flattening a possum crossing the road. Sheriff Grizzle's large square head hadn't even faded from view before a trio of vultures landed on the asphalt to partake of an unexpected *al fresco* lunch.

Thelonious turned away from the gruesome scene. As he inspected his camera for damage, he felt a playful tug on the back of his shirt collar. When he spun around to catch the party responsible, there was no sign of anyone. It was just the unlucky pedestrian and the two opportunistic vultures making quick work of it.

Hang on, hadn't there been a third?

The tugging grew more insistent. Swatting at his neck, Thelonious heard an irate squawk. It was followed by a foul-smelling gust as large wings beat the warm air. Suddenly the soles of his trainers were no longer touching the ground. Thelonious thrashed about, trying to free himself from the smelly creature's clutches. "Unhand me!" he roared, not caring how ridiculous he sounded to the scavenger that wanted to turn him into dessert.

A moment later Thelonious was back on the ground, his deerstalker hat lying upside-down beside him. The vulture took flight, but not without uttering one last piercing expletive.

Thelonious brushed himself off, doing the same to his cherished hat before returning it to its rightful place atop his head. He needed a wash and a change of clothes.

He stank of bird.

Chapter Six

FOR MOST FOLKS A TRIP to the gas station was just another chore, but not for Nate Jessop. At least not today. Today his new credit card had arrived and he was using it to fill the tank of his old pickup. As he watched the numbers on the pump ticking higher, Nate couldn't stop grinning. Before he'd only done unskilled jobs paying low wages, but now he was a professional man with a professional occupation. Maybe he didn't earn much more than he did at Joe's Hardware, but that was okay. He was finally on his way up—or he would be once he got the scoop on those bank bandits.

Nate had a lot of driving to do if he wanted to get through all those interviews he had planned and still be back in time to write up his copy for tomorrow's edition. The *Pinewood Times-Courier* came out in print once a week (as did the online version)—he needed to finish his story before he went home tonight or old man Clemson would bust a gasket.

Nate had spent most of yesterday on the phone chasing down leads and getting the same information. Sightings of a little person that looked like a bear had been reported in two neighbouring counties, one of which was his. He was convinced this individual had to be one of the bank bandits.

Since it was fixing to be a long day, he figured he'd better call his ma to tell her he wouldn't be home in time for supper. He'd catch hell from his pa, but that couldn't be helped. Nate was a professional newspaper reporter and that needed to take priority over being late for supper, even if it meant he had to wait a little longer to eat his ma's delicious fried chicken!

The first interview of the day was Zeke Oswald, a lead Nate got by cold calling the sheriff's department in the next county. Zeke—or *Ezekiel* as he preferred to be identified in the newspaper—worked at the front desk of a motor lodge off the Interstate. He tried to give the impression he was real important, so Nate played along, hoping he'd get something useful out of him.

"Soon's Ah saw the news on TV about that bank robbery, Ah called the police!" cried Zeke, making it sound like he was the big hero in all this.

His pink-rimmed eyes made Nate's water and he had to keep looking away to write in his notepad (or pretend to). Not that he had much to write. Zeke had nothing else to add except that the potential suspect was bad-tempered and drove an unusual car. "Cain't imagine why anybody would wanna drive around in a funny little thang like that," he recounted. "Heck, y'all couldn't even fit a shotgun in thare!"

Nate didn't fare any better with the next eyewitness—a bearded old crackpot in bib overalls that looked and smelled like they hadn't been washed since he'd bought them. As for that flea-infested beard of his, Nate got the heebie-jeebies just thinking about it. The old-timer went around with a shotgun strapped to his scrawny shoulder, ready to shoot if you even blinked the wrong way. His farm was so far off the grid it made the boondocks seem like a hopping place. It probably hadn't produced anything in years, unless you counted weeds as a crop. The barn was a wreck too, its roof half-collapsed from an oak tree that had fallen through it. As for the trailer the farmer called home, it was in worse shape than the metal dumpster Nate's sister Kimmie-Mae and her boyfriend Chester lived in with their kids.

Not that Nate had expected to be invited inside, but he was. He'd even been given some honest-to-goodness moonshine served in a jelly jar. It'd practically made his head explode! Nate had come across these "end of the world" survivalist types before, so he wasn't new to their ways. There were some in his town, though they lived on the outskirts, ready to defend their property against the coming invasion—those invaders usually being blacks or Muslims. If Nate's pa wasn't so goldurn lazy, he might've been ready too, but that would've meant having to get up from his stinky old recliner.

The farmer had called the sheriff's department to report a break-in at his barn. He'd described the intruder as a bear, whom he claimed wore a "funny" hat. As a matter of routine, they sent someone out to investigate. Not that anyone expected to find anything. Apparently the nutty old coot was famous in these parts and was always calling the sheriff's department about *something*. Nate heard he'd once claimed a UFO had landed on his property, though it'd ended up being nothing more extra-terrestrial than a paper plate someone had thrown from the window of a passing vehicle.

Unlike Zeke, the old-timer hadn't noticed what kind of car the "thievin' varmint" had been driving. "*Car?* How should Ah know what kind of car he was drivin'? Ah was too dang busy defendin' my property!" He shouted at Nate as if he were deaf. "Couldn't that dadburned critter *read*? Y'all kin see Ah got no trespassin' signs all over the place! Ah shoulda filled that furry hind end of his with a load of buckshot when Ah's had the chance! Woulda served him right, too."

Nate was getting pretty discouraged—and it got worse when he went to interview Dr. Bardeen, a general practitioner this bear person had gone to see. Nate's shoes didn't get any farther than the waiting room. The doc was way too busy to talk to him and instead referred him to the receptionist, who looked like she'd been sucking on lemons all day. Though she acted eager enough to talk, having already gossiped about the patient to her friend at the sheriff's department—the same friend who'd now become Nate's "source." He got the impression she hadn't exactly taken a shine to the patient. She wouldn't disclose his name due to patient confidentiality, but she had no problem telling Nate that he was foreign and had no health insurance, making both of these things sound like crimes.

"Ah could hardly understand a word he said from that accent! Y'all could tell he didn't wanna pay to see the doctor. Guess he's one of them socialists who wanna destroy our blessed American way of life!" She snorted with indignation. "He was a real weirdo all right. Grumpy, too."

Nate held back a laugh as he wondered if the receptionist might've confused the patient with Grumpy from "Snow White and the Seven Dwarves." Just last week he'd been reading it to his sister's kids while babysitting so she and Chester could go out drinking at a bar in the next town. They didn't get home till the next morning, having passed out in Chester's pickup in a KFC parking lot.

Having said all she was going to say, Dr. Bardeen's receptionist slammed her little window in Nate's face. By the time he left the doctor's office, he actually felt sorry for this bad-tempered foreign dwarf-bear, especially for having to deal with the receptionist, whose own grumpy temperament probably explained the lack of patients in the waiting room. If Nate had to get past her every time he needed to see the doctor, he'd prefer to stay sick.

Nate had better luck back on home turf with Pinewood County's tobacco-chewing Sheriff Maynard Grizzle. Sheriff Grizzle had been in office so many years folks had lost count. Nate regularly sought out the sheriff for information about what went on in the county, so it was plain old luck that he heard about this additional sighting. Not that Sheriff Grizzle had much to tell him, though he *was* able to provide one valuable piece of information—the car driven by the individual Nate was asking about had a Confederate flag on the roof. At last he was getting somewhere!

Although lots of folks flew Confederate flags outside their houses and still more had Confederate flag decals on their vehicles, Nate had never seen one painted on the roof of a car before. Maybe he'd keep this detail to himself instead of including it in his newspaper article, especially since he wanted to do his own detective work on the case. Heck, he had as much chance of tracking down the bank robbers as the local deputies. They seemed to be better at writing phoney traffic tickets or messing with other guys' wives than fighting *real* crime. Not only would Nate get the scoop, but he'd solve the crimes. He'd have his pick of big-city newspapers after that.

By the end of the day Nate was at his desk writing up his story, his spirits so high he caught himself singing. Even Miss Mandy, the paper's part-time office assistant and old man Clemson's niece, couldn't help noticing. She even brought him over a cup of coffee. "Ah thought this might come in handy," she said, offering Nate a wink that was part friendly and part something else. It was the *something else* that worried him. He thanked her politely, not wanting to be too encouraging since he suspected she was kind of sweet on him. It wasn't a good idea to get involved with the niece of the man responsible for his paycheque, especially knowing how emotional women could be. One minute they loved you, the next they wanted to chop off your nuts.

Although Miss Mandy was okay to look at, she already had a kid from back in high school—and she still hadn't lost the extra weight from that pregnancy. The kid's daddy had been older by two decades too. As Nate heard it, Miss Mandy's pa had run the feller out of town with a shotgun, though Nate suspected he'd run off on his own. Nate probably would've done the same. Lots of girls in school had got themselves knocked up, then tried to use the pregnancy to trap the guy into sticking around—girls like his sister Kimmie-Mae. As for Nate, he'd been smart and kept his fly zipped. Well, other than those times with Mindy-Lou Harris—and they didn't count since she couldn't get pregnant *that* way.

Gulping down the lukewarm liquid that passed for coffee at the *Pinewood Times-Courier*, Nate noticed that Miss Mandy had put in extra sugar. Did she think it would sweeten his feelings toward her? If so, she could forget it. He wasn't about to get mixed up with some girl right now. He needed to put everything into his career. If he didn't, he'd be stuck in this hillbilly shithole forever like his folks and Kimmie-Mae.

And Miss Mandy.

It was nearly eight at night by the time Nate finished filing his copy. He'd had to go over it again and again to make sure it didn't sound like he was accusing anyone of the robberies. Just because *he* thought this dwarf-bear had something to do with them didn't mean he could flat-out say so in print. He could only report on the information he'd been given, leaving readers to fill in the blanks. Old man Clemson had gone home ages ago, though Miss Mandy did offer to stay late in case Nate needed her. It had taken some doing to convince her to leave—and she only agreed to when he half-heartedly mumbled something about taking her to the movies on Saturday night if he had time. Not that Nate had any intention of actually going through with it.

Leaning back in his creaky chair with the vinyl cushion that had a split in the middle, Nate felt a real sense of accomplishment. He just wanted to sit here and savour the moment before he went home. He'd sure been thinking on his feet today, especially having the smarts to take a photo of Sheriff Grizzle with the newspaper's one and only digital camera, which he'd brought with him in case he dug up anything important and needed some art to go with it. Despite being busy, the sheriff suddenly became very cooperative when it came to being photographed. He'd even asked Nate to mail him a few hard copies of the newspaper when the article came out. Of course Nate had said yes. You had to keep your sources sweet!

Parking the tired old pickup in the Jessop family's cracked driveway, Nate entered the house through the screen door off the kitchen. The aroma of fried chicken perfumed the air, along with fresh-baked corn bread. Nate's mouth watered. His ma made the best fried chicken and corn bread in the world—even better than Luke's Diner. He hadn't eaten all day unless you counted that sugary cup of coffee Miss Mandy had fixed for him. As for the Snickers bar Nate had taken for the road, it'd melted into a gooey mess of chocolate, caramel and peanuts on the truck's dashboard, attracting a bunch of ants. He'd clean it up in the morning before heading to work. Right now he was too tired and too hungry to deal with it.

Nate had told his ma he'd be late and knew she'd put a plate of supper aside for him. The dishes, frying pan, mixing bowl and bread tin had all been washed and were now drying on the wire rack by the sink, signalling that his folks had already eaten. He smiled when he saw that the yellow Formica dinette table had been set with a cloth napkin along with a fork and knife and his favourite cup from Disneyworld, which a lady from church had brought him back from Florida a few Christmases ago. The oven had been left on the warm setting. Nate pulled open the door, practically drooling in anticipation of what was waiting inside.

It was empty.

He heard the TV blaring in the living room. It sounded like his folks were watching one of those amateur talent shows. Kimmie-Mae was always saying how she wished one would come to Georgia to hold auditions so she could try out, though Nate suspected Chester would have something to say about *that*. Although his sister could sing okay enough—or at least okay enough to get the kids to sleep—Nate didn't think she had what it took to get on television. Of course he'd never say as much to Kimmie-Mae; he didn't want to shatter her dreams. She had their pa and Chester for that.

"This here what they call singin' these days?" Earl

Jessop's voice cut into Nate's thoughts like a butcher knife cutting through meat. "Ah heard better comin' from a pig sty!"

Nate found his pa lying on his recliner, a beer can clenched in his meaty fist. Judging by the empties on the floor, it wasn't his first. His ma occupied a corner of the sofa, her posture as defeated as the crucified Jesus who'd once been nailed to the cross hanging on the wall behind her. "We-yall, look who's here?" said Earl in a sing-songy voice when Nate entered the living room. "It's Mr. Nathan Jessop, big-shot newspaper reporter! Y'all find out who killed Kennedy yet?"

A flush broke out on Nate's face and neck. Humiliated that his pa could still get to him like this, he turned away, only to see a plate of gnawed-over chicken bones on the end table next to the recliner. Since the Jessops never ate a minute past six o'clock, he knew that *this* was the supper his ma had set aside for him. Apparently Earl had hankered for a snack and decided to help himself to the contents of the warm oven, not even going to the trouble of switching it off. Mrs. Jessop looked at Nate with shame in her eyes before dragging them back to the TV screen, where a pretty young black girl had just finished her song to enthusiastic cheers and applause.

"Lord have mercy, she's finally done butcherin' that pig!" cried Earl, waving his beer can in the air. "My ears are bleedin' already!" He turned his attention back to Nate. "So what y'all gotta say for yourself, waltzin' on in at this here hour?"

Nate couldn't believe it. His pa was treating him like some teenager coming home drunk in the middle of the night instead of a grown man who had to work late. As for his ma, she seemed to be more scared and timid than usual, which worried him. He hoped his pa hadn't been knocking her around again. Maybe he'd better make sure he came home on time from now on, especially since late afternoon was when Earl started on his serious drinking. By the time he got nasty and felt like hitting something, Nate would already be there to head it off.

Although he was tired and hungry, Nate sat down on the sofa alongside his ma and stayed there until Earl passed out. Only then did he finally get up to brush his teeth and head to bed. A short time later he heard his ma doing the same as she shut off the TV and padded down the hallway to the bedroom she shared with her husband. He lay awake for nearly an hour listening for his pa to follow, but all was silent in the living room.

The next morning Nate was up and out of the house earlier than usual. His pa was still asleep on the recliner, snoring like a buzz saw. The living room reeked of stinky feet and stale beer. Nate didn't bother with his usual bowl of cornflakes, which he usually ate while standing at the kitchen counter. Although he knew it was a long shot, he thought he'd try to get a lead on those dwarf bank bandits by following the trail left by the "bear" one. It made sense to begin in the last place he'd been spotted. Maybe Nate might get the break he needed to kick his story into gear.

And to his surprise, he *did.*

Chapter Seven

IF ONLY HE HADN'T GONE looking for that church again.

Thanks to that irritating sheriff who'd nearly mowed him down with his patrol car, Thelonious's award-winning shot of the church trailer had one of his claws in it. Determined to replicate the image (minus the claw), he headed back the next morning. Alas, retracing his steps proved easier in theory than in practice. The rural landscape was beginning to look the same. Eager for a change of scenery, Thelonious could hardly wait to get up into the mountains at the northern end of the state. *Appalachia.* Even the name conjured up Southern magic and ancient myth.

The Appalachian Mountain Range was one of the oldest in the world. Aside from the obvious photographic opportunities, Thelonious thought he might have a go at camping and fishing while he was there. It couldn't hurt to get in touch with nature again. It would do him good to be reminded of his roots. Sometimes he needed to remember that most of his kind still lived in the wild, not crammed into dirty overcrowded cities trying to survive in a human world that only saw its own species as superior and worthy of life's many bounties.

Although Thelonious hadn't expected to socialise with his more "civilised" brethren in America, he knew they existed. They did the jobs no one else wanted to do, being exploited as cheap and disposable labour. He'd learned that large numbers of bears worked in the coal mines of Kentucky, West Virginia, Pennsylvania and other states. Some had even displaced the Mexican and Central American migrant workers in the West, particularly in agriculture, though working outside in the fresh air had to be preferable to getting black lung disease in some filthy pit. Apparently the United States was as unbothered about ursine rights as Great Britain. Maybe his life wasn't perfect, but Thelonious knew he'd had a lucky escape from a similar fate. Although he didn't have the required brawn to work in a coal mine, he couldn't imagine himself picking tomatoes either.

Forty minutes later with still no sign of the little church, Thelonious began to worry about other things—namely the changing light, which was why he'd wanted to be at the church around the same time as yesterday. Any later and the sun would wash away all those wonderful contrasts so essential to his work. He must've gone off course somewhere. At this rate he'd end up right back in the same town as that dreadful Dr. Bardeen and his Gestapo receptionist, not to mention the chatty veterinarian.

Thelonious had the lonely country road mostly to himself. Therefore he was surprised when a clapped-out red pickup truck suddenly appeared in his rear-view mirror, tailgating. These Southern drivers were really starting to get up his nose. Nevertheless, he wasn't about to exceed the speed limit just to placate some hillbilly with an ego problem, especially when he'd almost received a traffic ticket the day before courtesy of that dodgy sheriff. The road had been painted with a broken yellow line separating his lane from the oncoming one—there were plenty of opportunities for the truck to overtake him. When it didn't, Thelonious reduced his speed, hoping the driver would take the hint and go around him.

The pickup continued to ride on his tail, the driver's features hidden by sunglasses and a trucker hat. Sticking his furry arm out the window, Thelonious gestured with a come-hither motion known universally to every driver. "Pass, you blasted fool!" he growled. Instead the pickup slowed down, dropping farther and farther back until it disappeared from view. Perhaps it had turned off into one of the farms.

Thelonious had been so busy checking behind him for the truck that he almost drove straight past the church. The message on the sign had been changed since yesterday. It now said:

THIS CHURCH IS PRAYER-CONDITIONED.

A few minutes later Thelonious was squatting in front of the white trailer. He clicked off a sequence of shots, constantly examining the camera's viewfinder to make sure none of his claws had found their way into the images. As he finished up, a flash of red caught his eye. He squinted into the sunlight, seeing only farmland and the heat shimmering off an empty road. But as his vision adjusted to the brightness he saw something else.

Parked beneath a copse of trees was a familiar-looking red pickup truck.

The fur on Thelonious's neck prickled with warning. Was he about to become the victim of a robbery or carjacking? He could see someone seated at the steering wheel watching him, which was enough to send him scurrying back to the Mini, determined to add rubber to Sheriff Grizzle's offering.

The red pickup fell into place behind him, this time staying a few car lengths away. Not that Thelonious was fooled. Keeping his right paw on the steering wheel, he used his index claw from the left to tap in POLICE on the

SATNAV's touch screen. His paw shook so much he couldn't get past the first letter—which brought up everything from a pancake restaurant to a strip club with an extremely rude name.

The faster the Mini went the faster the pickup went until both vehicles were driving over the speed limit. Thelonious fought to keep the little car from careening into a ditch, though being lower to the ground the Mini Cooper performed better than the clumsy truck, which looked as if it were held together with electrical tape. Thelonious's mouth stretched into a smug grin when he saw it fishtail as it tried to chase him around a curve. The pickup struggled and sputtered, losing speed and giving Thelonious an opportunity to put some real distance between them. "Eat my dust!" he roared, jamming his wide flat foot down onto the accelerator pedal. The truck faded to a red speck.

Slowing to navigate a sharp curve, Thelonious saw a ranch. Its neglected pasture was occupied by a lone horse whose glory days were long past. It hung its head low to the weedy ground, too miserable to even twitch as flies used its back as a landing strip. Thelonious couldn't blame the poor creature for being in a sulk. He'd be in a sulk too if he had to stand about all day in a grotty field with nothing but a few crows for company. As the Mini came parallel, the horse lifted its heavy head and stared directly at Thelonious. Issuing a high-pitched whinny, its black lips curled back in a mocking grin, displaying a mouthful of large brown teeth. A baton-like phallus stuck out from its belly. To Thelonious's horror, it appeared to be getting longer. Suddenly the horse winked.

Thelonious sped away from the ranch, the awful whinnying echoing in his ears. Trying the SATNAV's search function one more time, he finally came up with the result he wanted. The driver of that red pickup would be in for a big surprise when Thelonious led him straight to the sheriff's department. As long as he was there, he'd get the phone number for the nearest glue factory.

He knew a horse that needed collecting.

Chapter Eight

NATE HAD BEEN ON HIS WAY to interview the bank manager that got shot in the foot by one of the robbers when a car with a Confederate flag on the roof showed up smack dab in front of him. It had to be the same car Sheriff Grizzle had told him about. The bank manager would have to wait. Heck, it wasn't like he'd be going anywhere, since he was still in the hospital. Nate had planned to take a gift basket of fruit to butter him up and get him talking. Obviously he couldn't take flowers or candy. If he did, folks would think he was queer or something.

The little car was whizzing along at speeds Nate's old clunker couldn't compete with, and he really needed to push the rattling engine of his truck to keep up. Half the time it struggled to reach 45mph, which was considered slow as molasses in these parts. Country folks thought nothing of riding your butt if you weren't driving fast enough for their liking. It was a power trip, especially when those dumb hillbillies like Kimmie-Mae's Chester were at the wheel. Those guys were always spoiling for a fight, but Nate had better things to do than get his nose smashed in by some dumbass redneck who couldn't spell his own name.

Nate followed as close as he dared. He tried to get a look at the driver, but all he could see was some dadburned hat—and it was on the passenger side. Whoever wore it must've been real short, which made sense if the car belonged to one of those dwarf bandits. As for the driver's side, it looked empty and so did the back seat, though just because Nate couldn't see anybody didn't mean nobody was there.

Worried he might've been too obvious, Nate eased up on the accelerator pedal, letting the little car get ahead. That was when he noticed the licence plate. It didn't look right. He figured it was fake, which confirmed his suspicions that he was tracking a real honest-to-goodness bank robber. Not long afterward he saw the car pull over in front of a white trailer, though when he got closer he saw that it was actually a Baptist church. Parking a few yards away under some trees, he sat in the comfort of his cab doing "surveillance work," putting to use the ancient binoculars that had been in the glove compartment. They were his pa's back from when he went hunting for deer—he'd probably forgotten they existed or he'd have sold them for beer money by now. Try as he might, Nate couldn't imagine Earl Jessop taking down a buck—not unless he could shoot one from his recliner.

Nate found a petrified stick of chewing gum in his shirt pocket and popped it into his dry mouth. It took a while to soften and release some flavour—not that there was much of it. He should've brought some bottled water with him or better yet, Gatorade. He had no idea how long he might be here—it could be hours. But Nate was new to this surveillance game; he couldn't be expected to get *everything* right. At least he'd worn his trucker hat. Guys wearing trucker hats and driving pickups blended into the Georgia scenery real good.

Training the binoculars on the car, Nate fiddled with the rusty dials to bring it into focus. The lenses hadn't held up too well over the years what with the binoculars being stored inside the truck during heat, cold and rain. Half the time it was like looking through lenses smeared with Vaseline. Suddenly the car door opened. Nate watched as a tubby little feller used some kind of contraption to lower himself down from the passenger seat. Except it wasn't the passenger seat at all—it had a steering wheel.

"Bingo!" he whooped, slamming the meat of his palm on the truck's cracked dashboard. Unfortunately, distance combined with his pa's crummy old binoculars made it impossible to pick out any facial features. The feller sure looked hairy though. Something about his hat seemed mighty familiar too.

Nate leaned forward, crushing his ribs against the steering wheel as he watched his surveillance subject aim a camera at the church. This went on for almost a half hour according to his Timex wristwatch, which had been a present from his folks on his eighteenth birthday. Although it had supposedly come from them both, Nate knew his ma had paid for it out of her wages from the diner. Convinced he was looking at one of the "animal dwarf bandits," Nate took a few photos of his own through the pickup's pitted windshield, zooming in as much as the *Times-Courier*'s cheap camera would let him. No way was he getting out of the truck for a better look. For all he knew, the rest of the gang could be sitting in that car with those old-fashioned gangster guns of theirs.

Not that Nate was dumb enough to actually confront anyone. The robbers were considered armed and dangerous, and he had his limits when it came to being a hero. He probably shouldn't have been following the little car in the first place. Old man Clemson would chew him out for it, but Nate needed to get the story and that's what reporters did— they took risks. Those guys over in Iraq and Afghanistan— they didn't let a few bombs or terrorists scare them away. They did what they had to do and so would he.

Nate made notes in his reporter's notepad, making sure to document every detail no matter how minor. The next time he looked up, his subject was doing some kind of fast-waddle back to the car, looking around like Lucifer himself was after him. Suddenly Nate realised where he'd seen the hat before. That famous Sherlock Holmes detective feller had one.

Ace reporter Nate Jessop once again found himself in hot pursuit, the truck's speedometer inching scarily past 70mph. The little car was going much faster this time and he wondered how long his old pickup could keep pace. Something was definitely up. Maybe the church was being targeted for a robbery and this feller had gone there to "case the joint." Why else take pictures? The church was nothing special. It was just a trailer with a cross on the roof. Could be those dwarf bandits had decided banks were too risky and wanted easier pickings—and robbing a church during Sunday service would be easy as pie. Folks dressed up in their Sunday best; for some this included jewellery. Then there was the collection plate. Nate noticed that parishioners seemed to be a lot more generous when others had their eye on them. Imagine how much cash, jewellery and credit cards they could steal—and at no risk to themselves? Well, unless someone brought a gun to church, which was always a possibility here in Georgia. Nate had seen plenty of folks bringing guns to church. Pastor Robinson never said a word about it either.

He wondered if he should tell Sheriff Grizzle what he'd seen. Because if something *was* being planned for this Sunday's service, at least the sheriff's men could be there to arrest the robbers before any real harm had been done—and Nate would be on the scene to cover the story. He could even ask Miss Mandy to come along to take pictures while he was busy doing interviews. Knowing her, she'd jump at the chance, especially if it meant spending time with him. Not only would Nate be a hero for helping to catch the bank bandits, he'd have the best newspaper article in the state. Even his pa wouldn't be able to come up with one of his mean cracks after that.

Nate didn't realise the sheriff's department was less than a mile away until he was almost on top of it. Now he didn't know what to do. His heart told him to keep following the little car, but his truck told him something else. Nate was pretty sure that clattering noise coming from under the hood hadn't been there earlier—and it was getting louder. The tyres weren't in the greatest shape either. The ones in back were practically bald. He'd been trying to save up to buy new ones, but with all the money he kept giving his folks every payday he couldn't afford it.

The squat building housing the Pinewood County Sheriff's Department was just ahead on his right. Suddenly the vehicle Nate had been pursuing swerved into the parking lot, going so fast it knocked over the sign for the upcoming 5K run. Stopping a few feet shy of the driveway, Nate watched as the car shot into a handicapped space by the front entrance. The next thing he knew the little driver was waddling up the ramp to the door. He seemed to be struggling with it, pushing and pulling until he finally got it open wide enough to squeeze through.

Nate drove into the parking lot, backing into a space alongside a patrol car. He shut off the engine. The height of his cab gave him a good view of the building's big plate-glass window. It was almost like being at the movies, with the window being the screen. He recognised Miss Sue-Ann, the wife of the department chaplain, standing in the window. Nate knew she stopped by regularly with a batch of home-made apple fritters for the guys. She was famous for them. Every time she brought some to the church bake sale they'd be gone before he could even get his wallet out.

Miss Sue-Ann moved off to the left until Nate could no longer see her. She was replaced by Sheriff Grizzle, who looked like he was talking to his feet. He had his hands on his hips in that irritated way he had, like he was sick and tired of dealing with someone. Nate had been on the wrong side of him a couple of times when he was a kid, both occasions for underage drinking. The sheriff didn't take kindly to young'uns and alcohol. He'd even been known to lock them up in a jail cell overnight if he thought it might do some good. Luckily, Nate had missed out on *that* part.

Sheriff Grizzle seemed to be getting more ornery by the minute. Nate sure wished he could hear what the sheriff was saying because he was definitely riled up about something. As for the driver of the little car, he was nowhere to be seen. Miss Sue-Ann had returned to the window, this time holding something wrapped in a napkin. She handed it to the sheriff, who disappeared from view, only to reappear at the door, where he gobbled down the contents of the napkin. Suddenly he opened the door, stepping aside so someone could get past. Nate expected to see Miss Sue-Ann coming out. Instead he saw the little feller with the Sherlock Holmes hat.

What in heck was he doing with Sheriff Grizzle?

Chapter Nine

"WHY, LOOKEE WHO WE GOT HERE?" greeted Sheriff Grizzle as Thelonious went trundling up to him. "It's the feller with the funny l'il car! Ah hope y'all ain't been makin' any more of them illegal yew-turns?"

"I'm here to report a crime!" Thelonious crossed his arms in front of his chest, trying to look authoritative.

"*A crime?* Is that so?"

The sheriff forgot all about Thelonious as a woman sashayed over with a basket of pastries. Smiling brightly, she fluttered her eyelashes at him like some *femme fatale*. Sheriff Grizzle's rough-hewn features softened into mush. "Miss Sue-Ann, y'all make the best apple fritters in the South!" he praised, shoving one into his tobacco-stained maw.

Thelonious had been given quite a fright—and he wanted something done about it. But the sheriff appeared to have more urgent matters on his policing agenda than protecting the public, such as stuffing his face with apple fritters and eyeballing the backside of the woman who'd baked them. Thelonious might as well have been having a conversation with himself as he recounted what had happened. "He's probably still out there!" he added.

"A red pickup?" echoed the sheriff, his chin speckled with crumbs. "Now that don't make no sense. Why would somebody be chasin' y'all?"

"How the hell should I know?"

Sheriff Grizzle gave Thelonious a dark look. "Did y'all cut him off? Folks around here don't like gittin' cut off when they's drivin'."

"I didn't cut anybody off!" protested Thelonious. "He was behind me the entire time. In fact, he even pulled over to watch me when—"

"Lemme git this straight. You're sayin' this here feller's been followin' y'all?"

"That's what I've been trying to tell you! Some madman—"

"Now y'all jus' calm on down thare a minute, hear?"

Planting his wide flat feet firmly on the dull linoleum floor, Thelonious glared up at the sheriff. "I *am* calm!"

Grizzle snorted. "Y'all don't look calm to me. Ah suggest y'all take a couple of deep breaths. Life's too short to blow a gasket, son."

Thelonious clenched his teeth, fighting the impulse to gnaw the man's leg off, though it probably tasted like tobacco spittle. He let out an exasperated breath, which the sheriff promptly misinterpreted.

"Better now?"

Thelonious nodded. He felt the same as before, only angrier. "So what happens now? Will you go after him?"

"Y'all jus' listen here, son. If'n Ah arrested every feller drivin' a red pickup truck, the streets would be empty!" explained the sheriff, chortling through a mouthful of masticated dough. He gave the fritter woman a long-suffering wink. She'd been hovering close by, eavesdropping on the conversation.

"Yes, but—"

"Like Ah jus' said, if'n Ah arrested everybody with a red pickup nobody'd be left in the county. Why, even my wife drives one and so does my neighbour, Homer. Come to think of it, Homer's ol' mama drives one and she's gone on…lemme see…ninety-one years of livin' on the good Lord's earth. Ain't that right, Miss Sue-Ann?" Receiving a nod of confirmation, he added: "Y'all want Ah should arrest her too?"

For a minute Thelonious thought the sheriff was referring to Homer, the dog he'd had the misfortune of meeting at the veterinarian's surgery. Indeed, the thought of the amorous cur driving a clapped-out pickup truck gave him his first real chuckle of the day, which Sheriff Grizzle also misinterpreted.

"*See?* Ah told y'all thare ain't nothin' to worry about! Folks here like to drive too fast for their own good. Always have. That feller probably wanted y'all to git out of his way."

"But he didn't even try to pass me! He just kept following. If you knew how fast we were going—"

The sheriff pounced. "Y'all been speedin'?"

Thelonious felt like a mouse caught in a trap. "No!" he quickly backtracked. "Of course not!"

"Sometimes our country boys like to have a little fun with folks from out of town. Y'all shoulda jus' pulled over and let him git on his way."

"Then how do you explain the fact that he was spying on me while I was taking photos?"

"*Spyin'?*" Sheriff Grizzle stared hard at Thelonious. "Y'all been drinkin', son?"

"No, I haven't been drinking!"

The sheriff replied with a grunt.

"I'm telling you, this character was actually chasing me!"

"*Chasin'?*" Grizzle shook his large square head. "That's plumb crazy! Y'all lettin' your imagination run wild. Folks in these parts don't go followin' other folks—and they don't go spyin' on 'em neither. Now Ah suggest y'all head on home and cool your heels a spell." Clapping a hand on Thelonious's shoulder, Sheriff Grizzle ushered him toward the exit. "And don't be doin' none of that speedin' around here neither. My men are jus' itchin' to write some tickets."

"But—"

"Things'll look better after a good night's sleep."

"But—"

The sheriff pulled open the door, letting in a blast of hot air. "Y'all go to church, son?" he suddenly asked.

"Well, no. Not really."

Sheriff Grizzle looked at Thelonious with pity. "We-yall, that thare's your problem! Y'all need to be doin' the Lord's work 'stead of bein' out thare lookin' for phantom pickup trucks! Now how's about y'all lemme git back to doin' my job?" Stuffing the last of the apple fritter into his mouth, he pushed Thelonious out the door. "Y'all have a nice day now, hear?"

"So much for protecting and serving the public," muttered Thelonious once he was safely out of earshot. No wonder everyone was armed to the teeth.

Clomping back to the Mini in his ill-fitting trainers, he heard the labouring sound of an engine on its last legs. A red pickup truck rattled out of the car park—and it looked exactly like the one that had been following him. Thelonious's first thought was to sound the alert. There might still be time to catch this nutter, if that proselytising sheriff moved his fat backside fast enough. Not that Thelonious could envision him moving *anything* fast enough to catch the bad guys, though the man had wings on his feet when it came to scoring another apple fritter. Sheriff Grizzle continued to loiter in the doorway stuffing his gob, Miss Sue-Ann a fritter-pushing butterfly fluttering at his side. Thelonious could still smell the freshly baked apple fritters. He'd kept hoping she might offer him one.

Although he'd made up his mind to wait in the car park until he felt safe enough to leave, he was already catching menacing looks from Sheriff Grizzle. Thelonious delayed his departure for as long as he could, fussing with his camera bag and re-adjusting the Mini's mirrors. With any luck the driver of the pickup had got scared off after seeing Thelonious with the sheriff. He was probably long gone by now, hunting for his next victim to rob or carjack. At least that's what Thelonious kept telling himself as he backed out of his parking space, jamming on the brakes before the Mini's rear end almost slammed into the SUV parked across from him, its driver having pulled out without looking. He recognised Sheriff Grizzle's fritter pusher at the wheel. Evidently she thought the JESUS SAVES decal on her vehicle's rear bumper would save her from her own stupidity.

Thelonious drove away from the sheriff's department with no further incident. A short time later he found himself standing outside a pleasant-looking diner that claimed to offer "Home Cookin." Suddenly he realised he was starving.

A Taste of Heaven held court on the main street of a small town that went by the rather uninviting name of Stumpville. Wedged between a bank and a feed store, the diner gave off a cheerful vibe. A sign in the window advertised the day's special: two pieces of fried chicken, sweet "tater" fries, fried okra, homemade biscuits and all the sweet tea you could drink. Thelonious was sold! Perhaps he'd go for a wander with his camera after he'd filled his belly. Stumpville *did* have a sort of sleepy Southern charm to it.

Thelonious made himself at home in a plastic-upholstered booth in a corner, the smell of fried chicken coming from the kitchen making his chops water. He appeared to be the only customer there. As he waited to be served, he noticed several crosses hanging from hooks on the walls. Not that this was unusual—he'd come across this kind of religious symbolism on display in many small businesses in the South. There was even a plaque over the door that featured the scriptural message:

BLESSED ARE THEY WHICH DO HUNGER AND THIRST AFTER RIGHTEOUSNESS: FOR THEY SHALL BE FILLED.

Finally a slender sixty-something dishwater-blonde in a waitress's uniform ambled over. "How y'all doin' today?" she greeted. As she reached up to pat the beehive hairdo shellacked onto her head, Thelonious wondered how much of the ozone layer had been destroyed by all the hairspray she used. The woman looked as if she'd been hired when John F. Kennedy was president. Even her uniform had a retro look right down to the notepad with pencil stub in a top pocket. A plastic rectangle pinned to her bodice identified her as "Miss Polly."

Thelonious already knew what he wanted—the fried chicken special.

"Y'all cain't go wrong with our fried chicken!" Miss Polly assured him, scribbling in her notepad. "Folks just *love* our fried chicken!" She bustled off to the kitchen, returning in a flash with Thelonious's sweet tea, which came in a large plastic glass packed full of ice cubes. He gulped down the contents in one go, suffering a brain freeze that caused his furry brow to pucker. Before he could ask for a top up, Miss Polly was already standing in front of him with the pitcher and a kindly smile. "Ah kin tell y'all ain't from around here. Am Ah right?"

Suddenly Thelonious felt homesick. He missed gentle green landscapes and misty mornings. He missed cups of tea at any hour of the day or night. Most of all he missed real pints served in real pubs. The American versions claiming to be pubs were often just noisy sports bars where the person tending bar didn't ask if you wanted your "usual," since he or she had no idea what your usual even *was*. On his first evening in America, Thelonious had gone into one of these establishments expecting to be served a proper pint, only to be overcharged for some second-rate ale that went into a glass considerably smaller than what he was used to. When he'd asked if there'd been a mistake, the bartender glared at him as if debating whether to call the police. Later as Thelonious was leaving, he overheard the man complaining to another employee that "the little weirdo" hadn't even left a tip. After that Thelonious decided to stick with places where the strongest drink on the menu was sweet tea.

"I'm from England," he finally answered.

The waitress's eyes went wide, taking on a cartoonish appearance. "*England?* We-yall, shut my mouth!"

Thelonious hid an ursine grin as he helped himself to his refilled glass of sweet tea, though this time he took it more slowly. He found the woman's reaction quite endearing and was glad he'd decided to come in for a meal.

"Why, Ah ain't never even been out of Georgia!" cried the waitress. Without warning, she leaned in so close Thelonious could smell her floral perfume, her voice taking on a conspiratorial tone. "But ain't England where all them Muslims are? They scare the blazes outta me!" She pressed a hand to her heart, looking skyward. "Praise Jesus, we better do somethin' about them and quick before they done kill us all! Bad enough one sneaked into the White House. Why, that man wasn't even born here!" She shook her shellacked head in disbelief. "Kin y'all imagine—a foreigner bein' president of the Yew-nited States?"

Thelonious had no idea what to say to that, so he said nothing. He preferred to avoid discussing politics, especially since no one was representing his interests. His futile attempts to enlist the aid of his local MP had taught him that his minority was so inconsequential it didn't even register as a blip on the political radar. No one was worried about the *bear* vote.

"Oh, but Ah didn't mean foreigners ain't good folks!" Miss Polly added quickly, possibly mistaking Thelonious's silence for displeasure. "So y'all havin' a nice time visitin' here in Georgia?"

Thelonious gave her a forlorn frown. "Not exactly." Before he knew it, the waitress had shimmied into the booth, her heavily made-up features a neon sign of sympathy.

"Now tell Miss Polly all about it!" she encouraged, her flowery scent competing with the fried chicken.

Thelonious had come in for a quiet meal; instead he'd

found an agony aunt. Yet he couldn't stop talking, his monologue going mostly uninterrupted apart from an occasional "Oh my lord!" uttered by the waitress. By the time he finished, his gruff voice was squeaking with tears. To his surprise, he felt better.

"Bless your heart!" Miss Polly's cartoon eyes welled up with moisture as she patted Thelonious's paw. "And shame on that Sheriff Grizzle for not doin' his job and helpin' y'all! That ain't right!"

A bell in the kitchen dinged. Miss Polly scooted out of the booth. "Ah'll be right back with that fried chicken!" she said, winking at Thelonious with a tear-filled eye.

As he watched her departing figure, Thelonious began to regret having mentioned Sheriff Grizzle by name, but it had come pouring out along with the rest of the story. He was probably worrying for nothing. Besides, after today it was unlikely he'd ever clap eyes on the waitress or the sheriff again.

Thelonious made quick work of his meal, even gnawing on the chicken bones to get any last bits of flavour when he thought no one was looking. He patted his belly, which was stuffed beyond capacity thanks to the addition of a wedge of peach cobbler with a giant scoop of vanilla ice cream on top (the ice cream a freebie from Miss Polly). Loosening the button on the waistband of his trousers, he was finally able to breathe again. If this kept up, he'd need to buy a new wardrobe.

Slipping a generous tip beneath the sugar dispenser, Thelonious clambered out of the booth. The waitress was nowhere to be seen, though he could hear her cheery voice coming from the kitchen. Camera in hand, he lumbered down the quiet street in search of interesting subject matter. His endless refills of sweet tea sloshed around inside his belly like water in a washing machine, making him regret not having used the toilet before leaving the diner. At the end of the block he turned back. Other than the feed store—which had a forced old-timey quality to it—there was really nothing worth photographing. Snapping a few half-hearted shots of the exterior, Thelonious returned to the car.

A Taste of Heaven hadn't attracted any new customers since he'd left, but the bank next door *had*. In fact, it seemed unusually busy for such a dinky town. At least two dozen people were queued up inside. Many stood by the wall, with some sitting on the floor. Meanwhile outside a small car had backed up onto the pavement, its rear end blocking the lobby entrance. The car looked like one of those Italian or Korean models trying to grab a share of the Mini Cooper market. The doors stood wide open; even the engine was still running. Talk about being in a hurry!

Thelonious headed north, eventually joining the road that would take him to the town of Repentance and Pastor Jehoshaphat Jones's revival meeting. As he zipped along in the Mini, he congratulated himself for having mastered driving on the "wrong" side of the road in a right-hand drive vehicle. If he could manage this without disaster, some silly tent revival should be a doddle.

Suddenly something feathered and ungainly darted out in front of him. Thelonious felt the car being pulled toward a muddy ditch as he swerved to avoid hitting it. Braking to a juddering stop, he rested his head against the steering wheel, his breaths coming in ragged chuffs as he considered how close he'd been to ending up nose-first in the mud. When he looked back up, he saw the instigator of his near mishap standing in the road, challenging him to have another go.

"Oi, rooster! I just ate your wife for lunch!" roared Thelonious, leaning on the horn for emphasis.

Raising its beak haughtily in the air, the bird did a Mick Jagger strut the rest of the way across the road. With a piercing yodel, it took off in a clumsy attempt at flight, heading directly toward the Mini.

A moment later a grey-green splat landed on the windscreen.

Chapter Ten

"Animal Dwarf Bandits" Rob Stumpville Bank!
—Front page headline from the *Tri-Counties Gazette*

WHEN NATE SAW THE *Times-Courier*'s number on the screen, he'd figured it was his boss. Old man Clemson *never* called unless it was important. But Nate couldn't hear a goldurn thing other than crackling, which was why he'd left his surveillance post outside the sheriff's department—so he could get a signal on that crappy cell phone of his. Boy, he was madder than a wet hen when he found out it hadn't been Mr. Clemson at all. It had been Miss Mandy wanting to know what time Nate was taking her to the movies on Saturday night. From what he remembered of the conversation, he hadn't committed to *anything*!

It was the same gang. Though unlike the last robbery with the goat-masked one running the show (and doing the shooting), this time the robber in the bear mask had taken charge. Nate was willing to bet that feller he'd been following had been on his way to Stumpville Bank and Trust to join his partners in crime, but wanted to set up an alibi first. Pretty dang clever, if you asked Nate. Because who'd expect a bank robber to be hanging around the sheriff's department right before robbing a bank practically around the corner?

By the time Nate got back to the parking lot, the little car with the Confederate flag was gone. As for Sheriff Grizzle, not only had he left for the day, he'd gone down to Florida and wouldn't be back till Sunday morning. Nate figured it had something to do with his wife—it usually did when the sheriff went to Florida. So it was just a handful of deputies wandering around drinking coffee and killing time. Had Nate been there an hour later, he would've seen all hell breaking loose. But he didn't even hear about the bank robbery until the next morning after it had already hit the news. Miss Mandy had just cost him the biggest scoop of his career.

Although he didn't usually work on weekends, the first thing Nate did was head over to Stumpville to interview eyewitnesses so he could write a follow-up article to someone else's story. He still had time before he needed to file his copy—he had to make every word count, especially since it would be a whole week before anything new he wrote saw the light of day. When he'd first started working at the *Pinewood Times-Courier*, Nate had been okay with the idea of writing for a newspaper that only came out once a week. Now it frustrated the heck out of him. Of course this was also the first time there was any *real* news to report. Usually it was boring stuff—an old-timer who'd kicked the bucket or a church that needed to raise money to fix the roof. So Nate had to keep coming up with angles to make his copy fresh even when it was stale. There was no telling what he might learn if he asked the right questions. He hoped today he had those right questions.

First on the list was Jake Sampson, the bank manager at Stumpville Bank and Trust. Sampson had been with the bank for twenty-six years, working his way up from teller. Nate figured they'd be carrying his corpse out soon, if being red in the face and a hundred pounds overweight were anything to go by. Unfortunately, the bank manager didn't have much to tell Nate that he hadn't already told all the other reporters yesterday—and even this, Nate suspected, had been carefully edited. Jake Sampson was a Southern redneck right down to his redneck soul, which was okay for the *Pinewood Times-Courier*, but not okay for say, an important newspaper like the *Atlanta Journal-Constitution*.

"Them bloodthirsty midgets should git the death penalty—and Ah wanna be thare to stick the needle in 'em!" bellowed Sampson, dragging a soiled hanky over his perspiring brow. "Ah ain't ashamed to admit that Ah started prayin' right then and thare. Y'all could tell that bear robber was itchin' to pull the trigger. Ah saw Lucifer in his eyes!"

When the bank manager paused to catch his breath, Nate thought he was having a stroke and nearly called out for help before Sampson picked up from where he'd left off.

"To think my poor wife was almost left a widow…. Praise Jesus, it's a miracle Ah'm still alive!"

Each time Nate tried to push for something more specific, he kept hearing the same hymn—Jake Sampson, the man who'd almost lost his life (despite hiding in his office watching the robbery from behind the safety glass of a locked door). Nate was getting nowhere. Maybe he'd get something newsworthy out of the bank tellers who'd actually come face-to-face with the robbers. But when he asked to speak to them, Sampson stopped him dead. "Everybody's too upset to go talkin' to any more reporters," he said, suddenly taking on the role of the big boss. "Ah'm payin' my staff to work, not gossip. Saturday's our busiest time, seein' we're only open half a day and all. Speakin' a which, Ah's gotta git back to work myself." With a clammy handshake, the bank manager escorted Nate to the lobby door, waiting there until he'd reached the sidewalk before returning to his office.

Nate reviewed his list of interview subjects. It was now a

lot shorter, having contained the names of the employees Jake Sampson had barred him from interviewing. That just left A Taste of Heaven, the diner next door to the bank. A waitress there had waited on a customer who not only closely matched the description of one of the dwarf bandits, but had been at the diner near the time of the robbery. To Nate's relief, she was thrilled to be interviewed about the mysterious dwarf-bear, though much of what she said was so contradictory that half the time Nate couldn't be sure she was talking about the same individual.

Polly DuKane supplied Nate with endless refills of sweet tea, answering his questions on the fly in between waiting on customers. "He seemed like such a nice l'il feller," she said at first, patting her blonde helmet of hair. "But sad too. Truth be told, Ah felt kinda sorry for him. He was awful upset. Plumb near broke my heart!"

But the next time she stopped by with the pitcher of sweet tea, her opinion had changed.

"Ah knew somethin' wasn't right the minute he came in. Some folks give off a peculiar air—and he was one of 'em. And the way he badmouthed our Sheriff Grizzle, who everybody knows is the finest sheriff in all of Georgia! That ain't right!"

Miss Polly refilled Nate's glass, her arm shaking with outrage as she finally delivered a guilty verdict. "And to go robbin' our bank like that? Why, Ah been trustin' my money to them folks since Ah was a girl! It just goes to show, y'all cain't trust them foreigners, even the ones who leave a good tip!" Winking at Nate, she added: "He sure did love our fried chicken though! Ah swear he'd been chewin' on the bones before Ah took his plate away. But then, everybody loves our fried chicken. Sure Ah cain't git y'all some? We got a special today—two pieces of fried chicken, sweet tater fries, fried okra, homemade biscuits and all the sweet tea y'all kin drink! Our peach cobbler's real good too! Owen made it fresh this mornin'."

Nate declined the offer, his bladder ready to burst from

the sweet tea Miss Polly had been pouring down his throat since he'd come in the door. A few more questions and he had all he was going to get out of the waitress. Thanking her for her help, he practically galloped to the restroom, his mind reeling with what he'd learned. By the time he left the diner, Nate had compiled a brand new picture of the bank robbery suspect: a depressed chicken-bone-chewing satanic foreign dwarf who looked like a bear. Yep. That should narrow things down.

On his way back to the truck, Nate suddenly realised he'd forgotten to ask Miss Polly if her fried-chicken-loving customer had been wearing a hat. She hadn't mentioned one, though it probably hadn't seemed important to her. But it was important to Nate—it could confirm if that feller he'd been following was the same feller who'd been at the diner before the bank was robbed. As he turned to go back, he noticed a TV news van parked outside Stumpville Bank and Trust. It hadn't been there when he'd left the diner. The station logo on the van identified it as a Fox News affiliate in Atlanta.

A black electrical cable snaked out of the van's side-panel door. It led into the bank, the lobby door having been wedged open with a steel box. Inside Nate could see a smartly dressed man interviewing Jake Sampson. Another man in jeans and a T-shirt filmed them with a camera mounted on a tripod. Two female tellers Nate had seen earlier waited nearby, ignoring the long line of customers that had formed at the now-empty teller windows. When the news reporter finished with the bank manager, he gestured the women over and began to interview them as well. Nate couldn't believe it—these were the same tellers he'd been trying to get interviews with!

Nate was sure glad he didn't have a knife on him because if he did, he would've gone over to the van and sliced through that dadburned cable. Suddenly he felt ashamed of himself. It wasn't like him to have such unchristian thoughts. Those TV news guys were just doing their job the same as he was. The story was bound to get attention. Armed gangs of dwarves robbing banks—especially dwarves wearing chicken, pig, goat and bear masks—didn't come along every day.

Upset as he was, Nate wouldn't humiliate himself by returning to the bank to beg that sweaty old Jake Sampson to let him interview the two tellers who were now giving interviews to the Fox News reporter. Guess they all figured Nate wasn't enough of a big shot. Maybe he should count his blessings the bank manager had spoken to him at all, although Nate's boss would probably agree that Sampson hadn't provided anything newsworthy. Though for sure he'd want to include some of the more colourful quotes, since they were exactly the kind of thing that hit home with their "demographic." With old man Clemson running the show, Nate sometimes thought he was working for *The Redneck Times* instead of the *Pinewood Times-Courier*.

Nate slouched in the cab of his pickup, leafing through his notes. It was hopeless. The Jake Sampson interview had been a complete waste of time. As for the one with Miss Polly, she'd tried to be helpful, but she hadn't actually *seen* any of the bank robbers robbing the bank. She'd only waited on a customer who looked like one of the robbers. The fact that this customer had been eating at the diner close to the time of the robbery helped, but it still wasn't enough. Although Nate believed in his heart this individual was one of the bank bandits, he needed more to go on. He needed to turn coincidence into *fact*.

As he drove away, Nate saw another TV news van coming toward him from the opposite lane. It pulled into the parking space he'd just vacated, which was right across the street from Stumpville Bank and Trust.

Chapter Eleven

THE BIG DAY HAD ARRIVED. Thelonious dressed for the occasion in a white long-sleeved shirt and navy-blue trousers. Although he considered adding a necktie to his ensemble or even a jacket, he quickly dismissed the idea. It seemed unlikely the male attendees at a religious revival meeting being held inside a tent would bother with ties and jackets, especially in this heat. Thelonious stood on his motel bed to check his reflection in the mirror above the dresser. He looked like a furry Mormon. All he needed was a stack of religious pamphlets.

No sooner had Thelonious joined the main road than he found himself stuck behind a slow-moving cavalcade of Harley Davidson motorcycles. They were probably heading to a biker rally, which would explain why so many were out and about on a quiet Sunday morning in the sticks. Despite the temperature, the burly bikers wore black leather jackets, though a few had opted for vests, showing off thick arms covered with tattoos. THE LORD'S DISCIPLES was emblazoned in white letters across their leather-clad backs with the symbol of a cross centred below. Still more riders came flooding in, forming a snaking trail behind the Mini Cooper. Every motorbike had a miniature flag with the bloodied HE IS RISEN! image attached to the handlebars.

Thelonious T. Bear had just become an official member of the Pastor Jehoshaphat Jones traffic jam.

As the bluish-grey haze of exhaust began to fill the little car, Thelonious closed the windows, preferring refrigerated air to the toxic fumes spewing from the Harleys' muscular tailpipes as yet another wave of motorbikes joined the sluggish traffic. He broke into an anxious sweat as these newcomers swerved past him, cutting into the queue ahead. The powerful roar of their engines became so deafening he couldn't hear his Charlie Parker CD—and he'd turned the volume as high as he dared short of blowing out the speakers. Even with the windows shut Thelonious couldn't shut his nostrils to the scorching stink of exhaust as the convoy of traffic inched toward a bullet-riddled road sign.

WEL OME TO R PENT NCE!

Thelonious's stomach gave a threatening lurch. The Harleys' exhaust fumes were a fine perfume compared to whatever was now coming in through the car's air vents. He held his breath, worried he might be sick all over his clean white shirt. It smelled like someone was cooking up a pot filled with dirt, rotten eggs and something else—something unwholesomely *organic*. As he came up to a pig farm, Thelonious realised what the secret ingredient was: porker poo.

Suddenly a HE IS RISEN! billboard rose up in all its gory glory. A red arrow was attached to the top, pointing toward a weedy field enclosed by a half-collapsed barbed-wire fence. A large canvas tent had been erected in the middle of the field, an AMERICAN CHURCH OF GOD MINISTRY banner draped above the entrance. A handful of concession booths had been set up outside. Thelonious hoped one of them sold cold drinks. A pint would've gone done a right treat, but he suspected beer wouldn't be on offer at a religious gathering, especially on a Sunday morning.

The sun blazed down on the carnival-like setting, glinting off the roofs of the vehicles parked in untidy rows in the field. As Thelonious approached the dirt driveway where all the Harley Davidsons were turning in, he noticed a sun-browned pensioner in an orange safety vest directing drivers where to park. A makeshift sign indicated it would cost ten dollars. The vendor's bag around the old man's waist bulged with cash. As Thelonious got closer, he saw that the parking attendant had a hunting rifle strapped across his chest.

The man waved at him to stop. "Ten dollars!" he barked at the window on the Mini's passenger side. No cheery Southern "How y'all doin' today?"—just an ill-tempered demand for money. Since he didn't seem inclined to go round to the driver's side, Thelonious had to unbuckle his seatbelt and crawl over to the passenger seat. He let down the window, the smell of pig shit hitting him full in the face. He'd barely got his arm out before the ten-dollar bill was snatched from his paw.

"Y'all need to park down yonder by that thare tree!" ordered the leathery old codger, pointing off in the distance toward a half-dead oak.

The tree had several broken branches that had already crushed a section of barbed-wire fencing—and Thelonious was being told to park his beloved Mini Cooper there? "But don't you have anything closer?" he asked, having noted that there was still plenty of room by the tent.

The old man's desiccated features were set in a permanent scowl. "Y'all gotta park over thare!" he shouted, fiddling irritably with his deaf aid. The thing looked so slippery with wax Thelonious wondered how it managed to stay in his ear.

"But—"

"Y'all lookin' to cause trouble?" The parking attendant glared in Thelonious's general direction, refusing to make eye contact. The effect was disconcerting, especially since they were almost nose to muzzle.

"No, but—"

"C'aint y'all hear proper?"

Suddenly Thelonious realised that the cantankerous old goat had a lazy eye—and not just one, but *both*. Perhaps this explained why he didn't see all those empty parking spaces near the tent. "Look, if it's a matter of paying extra—"

The parking attendant readjusted his hunting rifle, making the weapon more accessible. "Y'all gotta park down thare! This here area's reserved for V.I.P.s!"

A chorus of Harley Davidson horns had begun to sound behind Thelonious, some playing melodies. He recognised the Confederate anthem "I Wish I Was in Dixie." He also recognised the Christian hymn "Amazing Grace," though there was nothing forgiving or merciful about the colourful language being used by the riders as they encouraged Thelonious to get a move on. Gunning the Mini's engine, he sped off toward his *non*-V.I.P. parking space. Had it not been for that rifle and the intimidating presence of The Lord's Disciples, he would've reversed over the disagreeable old coot's foot.

Twenty minutes later an overheated Thelonious reached the tent. Along the way he'd passed pickup truck after pickup truck, most of them with gun racks mounted in their rear windows. Although trucks outnumbered cars, minivans, SUVs and even motorbikes, nearly every vehicle had one thing in common—decals and bumper stickers. Thelonious saw Confederate flag decals and American flag decals and JESUS SAVES decals. He saw NRA bumper stickers and pro-life bumper stickers and PROUD TO BE AN AMERICAN bumper stickers. But the message that shouted the loudest was the blood-spattered HE IS RISEN!

The V.I.P. parking section had filled up since he'd arrived. Two expensive-looking black RVs with AMERICAN

CHURCH OF GOD MINISTRY banners attached to their sides occupied a substantial chunk of the now-cordoned-off area. A fire-engine red Hummer sporting the vanity licence plate JPHTJONES was parked nearby; the Georgia-issue plate featured the state's peach logo with IN GOD WE TRUST at the bottom. A HE IS RISEN! decal had been affixed to the Hummer's side windows as well as on the rear bumper.

Apparently the star of the show had arrived.

Thelonious stopped at a concession stand to purchase an overpriced "large" cup of watered-down cola that contained more ice than liquid. He drained the contents in seconds, almost choking on a piece of ice. Although he could've done with a refill, he didn't want to get fleeced a second time. That long trek through the weedy field had done him no favours. His hat clung to his head like wet rubber, making his head itch. Even his fur felt matted and sticky. Good thing he'd used deodorant, not to mention cologne. The last thing he wanted was to attract attention by smelling like an animal.

A bespectacled young man dressed in a starched white shirt and black trousers stood guard outside the tent's entrance, which had been roped off to control the flow of traffic. At Thelonious's approach, he thrust out his arm, blocking him from entering. "Ticket?"

Noticing the semi-automatic handgun holstered to the young man's hip, Thelonious took a wobbly step backward. "*Ticket?*" he croaked.

"Y'all gotta have a ticket to see Pastor Jones."

Had Thelonious come all this way for nothing? "I didn't realise."

"Thare might be a few left. Ticket booth's down yonder back of the tent."

The last time Thelonious had been told something was "down yonder" he'd almost needed a taxi to get back. He trundled off to find the ticket booth, worried he'd miss the start time. Several dozen sweating people were already ahead of him in the queue and still more fell into place behind. They pressed forward as if they didn't see him, forcing his muzzle into the wide backside of a man with a high-powered rifle slung over a burly shoulder and a ruthless case of flatulence. The baggy seat of his work-soiled jeans aided in the distribution of the foul effluence like a blanket fanning a flame until Thelonious's eyes and nostrils were burning. If he had to stand behind old farty-pants much longer, he'd grab the man's gun and shoot him with it.

After shouting and waving at the woman in the ticket booth until she'd finally looked down and seen him, Thelonious was informed that the cost of admission was $29.95, plus a $3.95 facility fee. *Facility?* It was a flipping tent!

The place was packed by the time he got inside. The tent had been furnished with folding plastic chairs placed in rows with an aisle running through the middle. The only empty chairs were those by the entrance, which was technically the rear of the tent and well away from the stage. Thelonious claimed the last seat on the aisle. Unless he could make his way forward with his camera, he'd end up with nothing but photos of people's backsides. He'd only brought his stealth model with him, so when he saw everyone with cameras and mobile phones and even tablets, his heart sank.

The bloodied HE IS RISEN! image formed a backdrop for the small stage, having been reproduced onto a white PVC sheet that looked like something used to cover a dead body at a crime scene. Movable stairs had been placed at centre stage and at the sides. Several spotlights had been positioned at floor level, with still more hanging precariously from metal beams. A portable electric organ and chair held court to the right of the stage next to an AMERICAN CHURCH OF GOD MINISTRY sign. The sign's twin was on the left.

The sweltering day promised to become a lot worse thanks to the press of overheated bodies in the airless venue. Pastor Jones's ministry had rigged up enough loudspeakers to outfit Wembley Arena—why hadn't anyone thought to include some fans? Thelonious noticed the ladies in dresses and skirts fidgeting as they tried to unstick their thighs from their seats. He wondered how much human sweat had accumulated on the plastic surfaces over time and whether anyone cleaned them before each use. Good thing he'd worn long trousers. They'd be going straight into the laundry bag after this.

The stink of human sweat tainted the stifling air, competing with the sharper tang of metal and gun oil, though nothing could hide the smell of pig poo wafting into the tent. A number of men had brought shotguns and rifles with them; some even wore camouflage gear as if they'd just come from slaughtering some defenceless woodland creature. Georgia was one of the states that had expanded on the U.S. Constitution's right to bear arms, passing laws making it legal to take guns into public places such as bars, churches and schools. Try as he might, Thelonious couldn't imagine walking into a pub back home to find everyone armed to their eyeballs as they stood about drinking their pints. He tugged his deerstalker hat lower over his furry ears, unable to rid his mind of the image of his head mounted above a fireplace. Perhaps sitting in the back wasn't so bad after all. At least he was closer to the exit.

The tent buzzed with excited chatter, competing with the excited buzz of flies as they attempted to go for a swim inside the perspiring cups of fizzy drinks the worshippers had purchased from the refreshment stand. Suddenly there was an ear-splitting crack. Thinking someone had fired a gun, Thelonious was about to take cover beneath his chair until he heard a second less-threatening crack, which gave way to a droning male voice whose owner sounded as if his mouth had been stuffed full of stones. A quick tempo started up at the organ. Pastor Jehoshaphat Jones's revival meeting was about to begin.

A solitary spotlight came on, illuminating the organ and a frumpy brunette whose head was too big for her body. Thelonious recognised the pastor's wife—she'd been on the cover of one of the American Church of God Ministry booklets being sold for a king's ransom outside the tent. She didn't look like a very good match for Pastor Jones, who—at least in his photo—brought to mind Hollywood actor George Hamilton in his heyday, whereas Mrs. Jones was as far from Hollywood as one could get. Her poufy hairstyle was at least two generations out of date and made her already oversized head resemble a balloon. The knee-length brown dress she wore amplified her dowdiness, showing off a pair of stocky calves, which disappeared into low-heeled brown pumps that made her feet seem huge. It was as if the woman had gone out of her way to look as unappealing as possible.

The pastor's wife managed to coax a lot of action from the little organ. It sounded as though an entire band shared the stage with her, including percussion and horn sections. Thelonious had been expecting a few lethargic hymns, but the music was 1970s Las Vegas Elvis with some extra corn thrown in. He kept waiting for the King to come bounding out on stage wearing some bejewelled monstrosity. But a man with shoe-blacked hair appeared in his place, opening his arms in Christ-like greeting as every spotlight in the house lit up the stage.

The audience went wild. Ecstatic shouts of "Praise the Lord!" and "Hallelujah!" filled the tent as everyone jumped to their feet and waved their hands in the air. Even the wheelchair-bound were spinning on their wheels in the aisle like boy racers. Thelonious's view of the stage was completely blocked. He had no choice but to stand on his chair or risk being made a casualty of a religious mosh pit.

Jehoshaphat Jones looked like his photo right down to the fake tan and strategically placed grey at his temples. "Praise Jesus, Hallelujah!" the pastor sang into his headset microphone.

Cheers and screams were returned, along with copious praisings of Jesus. Several women had begun to weep, alternating between hugging themselves for comfort and flinging their arms in the air in spiritual ecstasy. Even some of the male bikers had gone all teary-eyed, swiping at their eyes with beefy fists. The congregation's reaction to the arrival of this middle-aged messiah was so over the top Thelonious kept expecting to see women tossing their knickers onto the stage as their younger counterparts flashed their mammaries. The only thing missing was an electric guitar.

Apparently Pastor Jones had decided not to follow his wife's lead in the fashion department, preferring flash over frump. He'd dressed in an electric-blue satin shirt with black jeans and shiny black half-boots with steel tips. A wireless body pack transmitter was clipped to his black belt. He flung his arms high in response to his followers, his face beaming with a smile as artificial as his tan. Even his teeth looked fake. *A cap job for sure*, mused Thelonious, taking pride in his own naturally flawless choppers.

"Praise Jesus, Hallelujah!" cried Jehoshaphat Jones, inspiring yet another wave of animated shouting, cheering, weeping and clapping. The din became so deafening Thelonious had to clamp his paws over his ears, which provoked dark stares from his neighbours. No wonder the ministry had decided to hold the event in the middle of nowhere—anywhere else and they'd be breaking every noise ordinance in existence. Even the pastor's wife got in on the action, rising from her chair and casting up her shapeless arms, adding her own cheers to the hysteria. Dabbing at her eyes with a tissue, she sat back down at the organ to resume the musical corn. The women in Thelonious's row had begun to cry. He felt like crying along with them—his eardrums were killing him.

Finally everyone calmed down and resumed their seats as the music came to a resounding finish. "Let us pray!" instructed Pastor Jones, clasping his hands together and bowing his head. The tent fell blissfully silent, though Thelonious heard a ringing in his ears he hoped wouldn't be permanent. The crowd followed the pastor's lead, waiting until he issued an "Amen," which they dutifully repeated. Thelonious caught several worshippers giving him dirty looks for not having joined in the mass prayer, though he'd been the recipient of unfriendly glares ever since he'd first arrived, especially from the older ladies.

The next hour was taken up with a sermon consisting of readings from the scripture accompanied by many more cries of "Praise Jesus!" and "Hallelujah!" from both the pastor and his congregation. Sin seemed to be the order of the day and Jehoshaphat Jones had copious examples with which to caution his flock against, the more egregious of these provoking an ominous chord from the organ. Rather than stirring Thelonious to the religious fervour it did others, Pastor Jones's predictions of hellfire and brimstone were sending him to sleep. If this kept up, he'd be out like a light, hibernating into next spring. Other than this Jones character posturing about on stage with his Bible, there wasn't anything worth taking a photo of.

Until a young man stepped up onto the stage and handed Jehoshaphat Jones a snake.

The crowd issued a collective gasp. Thelonious perked up instantly, his claws curling around the stealth camera inside his trouser pocket. Maybe the day wouldn't be a complete washout after all!

As Mrs. Jones banged out some chords on the organ, Pastor Jones danced around with the snake, waltzing from one end of the stage to the other like a reptile-enamoured Fred Astaire. The two looked so cosy together Thelonious expected the pastor to break into a chorus of "Cheek to Cheek." Holding the creature's face close to his own, Jones appeared to be on the verge of kissing the thing but instead turned toward his audience. "Behold, I give unto you power to tread on serpents and scorpions, and over all the power of the enemy!" he proclaimed in a falsetto voice. "And nothing shall by any means hurt you!" He raised the snake high above his head.

The pastor's followers leapt up from their seats and flailed their arms about in a choreographed ballet of spiritual madness. A blast of smelly armpit drifted toward Thelonious, followed by an elbow hitting him in the head, knocking his deerstalker hat askew. Suddenly Pastor Jones was sprinting down the centre stairs with his serpentine companion. He stood for a moment surveying his flock, the snake curled cosily around his left forearm, looking either half-asleep or drugged.

"Praise Jesus!" Jehoshaphat Jones cried into his headset, sparking off the rote response. He began to move smoothly up the aisle like a dignitary stopping to shake hands, except it wasn't hands that interested him. With his snake-free arm, he slapped the meat of his palm against the foreheads of worshippers who'd stepped forward for what seemed to be some kind of blessing. They fell backward onto their neighbours, their bodies juddering as if a bolt of lightning had struck them. Thelonious couldn't believe what he was seeing. Either a large number of epileptics were in attendance or this smarmy preacher had given these people brain damage.

Stepping into the aisle, Thelonious got stuck in with his camera, capturing as much of the action as he could, debating whether he should try to get closer. Pastor Jones moved on to a heavyset woman balancing on a pair of wooden crutches, at which point the lethargic snake became more animated. "In My name they will cast out demons! They will speak with new tongues! They will take up serpents!" intoned the pastor, pausing for the sake of dramatics. "And if they drink anything deadly, it will not hurt them! They will lay hands on the sick, and they will recover!" His palm shot forward, making contact with the woman's shiny forehead. The congregation roared. Thelonious feared a riot would break out—and he didn't fancy his chances of survival.

The crutches clattered to the ground as the pastor's follower raised her flabby arms high in the air. She kicked the wooden sticks away with all the athletic dexterity of David Beckham, launching them clear across the aisle, where one clipped the ankle of an old man whose grimace of pain could be felt even by Thelonious. She began to dance a jig, wailing and praising Jesus now that her infirmity had been cured. Aiming his key-fob camera at the scene, Thelonious caught the hysteria on the worshippers' faces and the evil grin of the snake as it coiled itself tighter around Pastor Jones's forearm.

The creature was yellow and brown with a ridged tail. Although no expert on reptiles, Thelonious had watched enough wildlife programmes on telly to make an informed guess: Jehoshaphat Jones's slithery sidekick was a rattlesnake.

The pastor continued to make his way up the aisle toward the back, offering the occasional head-bashing to parishioners. As he reached the last row, he came to a stop directly in front of Thelonious. The snake chose that moment to open its mouth wide, displaying two needle-sharp fangs. Fixing its tiny eyes on Thelonious, the reptile's forked tongue slithered in and out in an obscene parody of a kiss, whereupon Pastor Jones's artificial smile grew even more saccharine. His capped teeth were like the white keys on a piano in the fake-tan darkness of his face, which looked far more middle-aged than it had in his photo. Aside from being deeper, the creases at his eyes were noticeably lighter in skin tone than the surrounding facial tissue. Thelonious suspected a bad tan job or a cut-rate eye job.

Jehoshaphat Jones observed Thelonious like a hunter trying to fool his prey into thinking it was safe from harm. Suddenly he leaned forward, the snake leaning along with him. Thelonious could actually smell the creature's breath, which reeked of half-digested rodents and other things he dared not imagine. He felt his bowels loosening as the duo came closer. When he tried to take a few steps back, he found his way blocked by his neighbour with the rancid armpit and sharp elbow. The pastor's smile was so wide Thelonious could see the back teeth.

"Behold, I give unto you power to tread on serpents—"

Thelonious felt the shutter click as he pocketed his tiny camera, hoping it hadn't been seen. Darting past the pastor's legs, he took off in a toddling run toward the wholesome sunshine outside the tent. He kept expecting a hand to grab his shirt collar and pull him back inside, but no one tried to stop him. Ducking behind the refreshment stand, he gulped in the hot pig-shit-scented air, which now smelled as sweet to his ursine nostrils as spring wildflowers. The weed-ridden field was chock-a-block with cars, pickups, minivans and RVs; there was even a rickety old bus. But no one was in sight, not even the crotchety parking attendant. The vendors had abandoned their booths as well. They'd probably all gone inside to watch the freak show.

The Mini's Union Jack blazed like a rescue beacon in the sun. Thelonious hurried toward it, constantly checking over his shoulder to make sure no one was behind him. He almost expected the car to be gone by the time he reached it, disappearing like a mirage. Even after he'd locked himself inside he kept patting the dashboard and steering wheel to reassure himself they were real.

Thelonious kept seeing the snake grinning in at him through the windows. He even saw it coiled up on the back seat, waiting to strike. Suddenly he noticed stains the colour of rusty piss all down his white shirtfront. They hadn't been there earlier. In fact, they hadn't been there until that filthy creature had come near him. This was the last time he'd put himself in harm's way for the sake of a few images. If he'd wanted to risk his life, he would've become a war photographer. At least it was more ennobling than being Sunday lunch for some spray-tanned preacher's pet snake.

As he exited the dirt driveway, Thelonious saw the CHURCH SERVICE sign. The folding panel had been placed in the middle of the road. One lane was already half-blocked by a patrol car, making it impossible for two vehicles coming toward each other at the same time to get safely past. A man in a uniform and hat leaned against the side of the patrol car, his broad jaw working enthusiastically. As the Mini approached, he tossed what appeared to be a hip flask onto the front seat and removed his hat. Thelonious would recognise that large square head anywhere. Unfortunately, it was too late to take evasive action. Not only had he been spotted, but he was being motioned at to stop.

"Why, lookee who we got here!" greeted Sheriff Grizzle, sauntering over.

Thelonious let down the window, nearly gagging from the

barnyard stench. Just his rotten luck to have landed on Grizzle's rednecked radar. "Hello, Sheriff."

"Ah see y'all's been at the big revival meetin'." The sheriff's mouth was so flooded with tobacco spittle Thelonious expected it to pour down his chin like sewage from a broken main. Instead Grizzle bestowed it onto the asphalt. "Funny, but Ah didn't have y'all pegged as the church-goin' type, 'specially after our last conversation."

"How did you know I was there?" Thelonious didn't bother to hide his growl.

"Saw y'all leavin'." The sheriff checked his wristwatch. "Is it over already?"

"I left early."

"Not innerested in the Lord's word?" Leaning in through the open window, Sheriff Grizzle added his tobacco and booze breath to the scorching pig-shit-scented air. "So Ah hear tell y'all been complainin' about me."

"Complaining?"

"Yep. Guess y'all ain't too happy Ah didn't use police resources to go off on some wild goose chase to find your mysterious pickup-truck feller." The sheriff shook his large head, awakening a few flecks of dandruff. Thelonious watched in horror as they floated into his lap, standing out like greasy snowflakes against the navy blue of his trousers. "Seems like every time we git outsiders comin' into our county they do nothin' but cause trouble."

"But I haven't been causing—"

Sheriff Grizzle's expression hardened. "Now Ah already done told y'all once it ain't illegal for a feller to go drivin' his own vee-hicle on a public road, but Ah reckon my word ain't good enough. Naw. 'Stead y'all had to run off carpin' to anybody with a set of ears. Folks in these parts count on me to do right by them, so when Ah hear somebody's been badmouthin' me Ah ain't too happy about it. We don't take kindly to troublemakers around here."

The sheriff must've been referring to that waitress at the diner Thelonious had eaten at the other day. He knew he shouldn't have talked so much. The next time anyone started that "bless your heart" nonsense, he'd keep his big fat gob shut! "Speaking of things *illegal*, they've got a rattlesnake back there." Thelonious indicated the weedy field. "Someone could get hurt. In fact, I nearly got bitten myself. See?" He pointed to his stained shirtfront. "That's snake venom!"

"A rattlesnake?" Sheriff Grizzle scraped his chin with a stained thumbnail. Suddenly he grinned. "Y'all want me to arrest it?"

"But this is serious!"

"Naw, c'aint be no rattlesnake. Y'all must've seen one of them rubber thangs the young'uns like to play with."

"I can assure you, it was *not* made of rubber." Squaring his furry shoulders, Thelonious added: "Isn't it illegal to use a snake in a religious service?" Although no expert on American law, he knew dodgy when he saw it.

The sheriff looked taken aback by the question. "We-yall, it is and it ain't," he finally answered. "Church folks here in Georgia need a special permit for snake handlin'—and Ah ain't heard nothin' about no permits bein' issued."

"I know what I saw. And I saw a snake."

"Like Ah said, Ah ain't heard of no permits. So that's why what y'all thought was a snake c'aint have been a snake. See?"

"Actually, no."

A dribble of brown juice leaked from the corner of Sheriff Grizzle's mouth. He wiped it away with his sleeve, leaving a diarrheal stain on the khaki fabric. "Listen close, son. If'n y'all saw Pastor Jones with a snake and it's illegal for him to have a snake, then y'all c'aint have seen a snake. It ain't rocket science!"

The sheriff seemed determined to gaslight Thelonious with some bizarre country logic. Maybe he was on Jehoshaphat Jones's payroll? "I must've been mistaken then," mumbled Thelonious.

"Y'all sure got a lively imagination. But y'all still didn't see no snake," Grizzle reiterated, looking angry. "This here county's full of honest God-fearing folks. We don't like troublemakers comin' here stirrin' things up. And that includes troublemakers who got a habit of runnin' off at the mouth." The sheriff whacked his palm on the Mini Cooper's roof. "Now git!"

Thelonious was more than happy to "git!" The sooner he saw the back of Sheriff Grizzle's precious county, the better.

That night at his motel Thelonious transferred the handful of photos he'd managed to take at the revival meeting onto his laptop, not expecting to find anything of use—*until* he came to the last image. A yawning reptilian mouth showed off two curved fangs, their tips glistening with a drop of yellowish liquid. A fuzz of human faces in various states of religious hysteria filled the background. When had he taken *this*? Suddenly Thelonious recalled the shutter going off right before he'd hidden his camera in his pocket. The best photograph of his career—and it had happened by accident.

Not long afterward Thelonious dozed off in front of the television, doing so just as a face he would've recognised came on the screen. Speaking to a news reporter was A Taste of Heaven's Miss Polly. She had quite a story to tell about a customer she'd waited on before Stumpville Bank and Trust had been robbed.

"Praise Jesus, Ah'm lucky to be alive!" she cried, patting her shellacked blonde beehive, her expression zigzagging between terror and gaiety. "He seemed like such a nice lil' feller. Ate up everythin' on his plate too. He sure did love our fried chicken. But then, *everybody* loves our fried chicken!"

Chapter Twelve

THE RESIDENTS OF STUMPVILLE were in a tizzy about the Dillinger-style bank hold-up that had taken place in their quiet little town with a population of just under two-hundred, a few of whom—despite having been counted in the last census—had four legs. The mayor had a reputation for being creative when it came to getting government funding for his rural fiefdom, which likely explained how he'd held on to his office for so long. What did it matter if Duke the coonhound or Marmaduke the pit bull terrier had been counted in the population figures? They were legitimate residents of Stumpville too.

The bank robbery was the biggest thing to hit Stumpville in the town's history. Even the old-timers who'd been part of the scenery for as long as anyone could remember agreed that the armed heist at Stumpville Bank and Trust outshined even the time former Georgia governor turned U.S. president

Jimmy Carter visited during the big oil crisis of '79. Not that it was much of a contest. Locals hadn't voted for the peanut-farming Democrat anyway. The town had always been heavily Republican (except for the canine residents, since they hadn't registered to vote).

Although the small-statured individual who'd enjoyed a fried chicken special at A Taste of Heaven just before the robbery was only considered a "person of interest" rather than an actual suspect, the residents of Stumpville had already reached a guilty verdict. The townspeople wanted to bask in their notorious glory for as long as possible, especially since curiosity seekers from other parts of the state had begun to show up on the streets of Stumpville, which translated into money being spent at local businesses.

Anticipating a wave of tourism, A Taste of Heaven added the "Bank Robbers Special" to their menu. It consisted of two pieces of fried chicken, sweet "tater" fries, fried okra, homemade biscuits and all the sweet tea you could drink. Not wanting to be outdone, the feed store added T-shirts to their range of apparel, which until now had been limited to waterproof rubber boots, gardening gloves, trucker hats and Fruit of the Loom men's boxers in plastic-wrapped packs of four (white only). These specially made Tees featured the cartoon image of a bear holding a Tommy Gun, with STUMPVILLE GEORGIA printed in easy-to-read block letters beneath. The feed store's owner planned to expand the line to include images of the goat, pig and chicken bandits, but he wanted to see how well the first design did before he invested more capital.

Although not the first town in the state to get hit by the "animal dwarf bandits," entrepreneurial Stumpville had what its competition did not: Mayor Jarvis Calhoun.

Mayor Calhoun had plans. *Big* plans. It was all well and good to sell a few T-shirts or a plate of fried chicken to a few nosy parkers from out of town, but the mayor had bigger fish to fry. He wanted to attract film and television production companies to his little hamlet. He didn't care what they wanted to produce—zombies, vampires, werewolves, housewives…. As long as none of them heathen pornographers or hip-hopping thugs came a calling, Stumpville was open for business! Why should Atlanta and its nearby cousins get all the action?

Of course Mayor Calhoun had plans for himself, too. He wanted to run for governor of the great state of Georgia. But until Stumpville claimed its rightful place on the map, he didn't have a hope on God's green earth of it happening. Although state politics was chock full of good ol' Republican boys like himself, they usually came from places folks had actually heard of. The mayor intended to change all that. Not that he expected to turn his humble little town into another Hollywood or even another Atlanta, but he'd sure give them a run for their money.

So Mayor Jarvis Calhoun went from being a paper-pusher and rubber-stamper to being the town's official publicist and P.R. man. He invited reporters from every newspaper in the state, not to mention every TV station to come to Stumpville to report on the big bank heist, even offering a personal interview as part of the package. Although he was always happy to see his name in print, what he *really* wanted was time in front of the television cameras. Of course he didn't expect every reporter in Georgia to come running—it was more a matter of casting the rod to see how many fish would bite. He'd had to do some fancy footwork to make it happen, reallocating funds so that the mayor's office could pay for motel rooms for those reporters who'd had to travel longer distances. Good thing there was a respectable motel on the main route outside of town and still another heading out toward Repentance.

Not that the mayor wanted to condemn any of his fellow good Christians to a night in Repentance, Georgia. The town—if it could be called a *town*—was a bunch of pig farms with an abandoned railroad depot and used tractor dealer thrown in. Folks always knew they were heading in the right direction by the smell of pig dung. Mayor Calhoun's wife came from Repentance—and straight off a pig farm, too. He should've known better, but being young and foolish, he'd let his hormones lead him to the altar. Now he was stuck with the woman until the day he died. Or she did.

And he knew which option he preferred.

Repentance was the perfect place for the likes of that no-account snake-wrangling heathen Pastor Jehoshaphat Jones and his heathen followers. Mayor Calhoun didn't approve of such shenanigans being carried out in the name of the Lord. That American Church of God Ministry was no church he'd be tithing anytime soon, though he'd found out that his wife had opened her pocketbook to them a few times since her folks were members. He'd put a stop to that real quick, especially since it was *his* money she'd been filling their blasphemous coffers with. He wished they'd take their revival meetings someplace else instead of conducting them practically on his doorstep. Bad enough having that useless drunk Maynard Grizzle turning a blind eye to what went on in his own county—and Jarvis Calhoun wasn't so green as to not know the reason behind *that*. Sheriff Grizzle was as crooked as they came, though the mayor had no cause to complain when it suited his own agenda. Although almost all of Stumpville was of the Faith (and there was only *one* Faith), he still had a professional obligation to hide his prejudices against the occasional Pentecost, Catholic, Jehovah's Witness or Episcopalian who lived within the town limits. Thankfully these dissenters were few in number and didn't include Mormons, Jews, Atheists or any of them Muslim fanatics who wanted to destroy the great American way of life.

Jarvis had held up well for his age, but his wife had gone to pot way before she'd hit thirty. With each birth of their three daughters, she got wider and lazier and stupider. She now spent all day watching those women's programmes and soap operas on TV and stuffing her face with junk food. On a good day she'd have dinner waiting for him on the stove when he got home, though it was usually Hamburger Helper or something else that could be prepared out of a box. On a bad day she'd be buried up to her triple chins beneath the bedclothes with one of her "headaches." The mayor couldn't even remember the last time he'd seen her get gussied up— probably not since he'd been re-elected! He wondered if she had some kind of depression, though what she had to be depressed about he couldn't for the life of him imagine. The girls were all grown up and had their own families to take care of, so the stress that went with childrearing couldn't be the problem. His wife lived in a nice house filled with nice furniture; even her Chevy SUV was only a year old. She didn't have to work. She didn't have to do much of *anything*.

Depression or no depression, the mayor figured his wife was just one of those women who enjoyed feeling sorry for herself all the time. She probably got it from all those TV shows with the yapping females who were always finding something to whine about. Jarvis didn't intend to push the depression issue. She was the wife of a mayor in a small town where everybody knew everybody else's business. It wouldn't look good for him if she was popping pills for some mental problem.

Nevertheless, Mayor Calhoun was worried. What would happen once his big plan began to fall into place? Because if his wife was this much of a liability now, things would only get worse when he ran for governor. Maybe he'd get lucky and she'd eat herself to death before then. A widower running for governor would definitely get the sympathy vote. Too bad he hadn't married Polly DuKane years ago when he'd first had the chance, though everybody had said she was way too old for him. Even now she was way too old for him, but she was still a damned sight better than his wife.

Everyone loved Miss Polly. So it came as no surprise that Stumpville's favourite waitress was well on her way to becoming a minor celebrity, thanks to being interviewed by news reporters who'd come to town to cover the story. Other than the employees and customers in the bank during the robbery, Miss Polly was the only person who'd been in close proximity to one of the supposed "animal dwarf bandits," let alone had a conversation with him. She was enjoying her moment in the sun almost as much as Mayor Calhoun. Her ageing face glowed from the attention as well as from the new sun-bronzing powder she'd bought in the cosmetics department at the Walmart a few towns away. She'd even started to use a more vibrant shade of hair colour to liven up her dishwater-blonde beehive. These changes had taken at least ten years off her age—and this didn't go unnoticed by the mayor's nostalgic eye. Even Jake Sampson from the bank had started giving her looks, though Miss Polly wasn't about to go fooling around with some married man, especially one whose wife was not only a very dear friend of hers, but went to the same church. Anyhow, she couldn't picture herself being with someone his size. Not that she expected George Clooney to walk into the diner and sweep her off her feet, but Jake Sampson? Lord have mercy!

The Gulf War had made Miss Polly a widow in her forties. After that she'd pretty much given up hope of finding a man again. It was slim pickings in a small town like Stumpville, especially for women *her* age. The only "eligible" bachelor was Jed Pickett, the crazy old feller who lived in a trailer at the edge of town—and he was so ugly he'd scare a buzzard off a gut pile. He'd had a leg blown off in Nam too. Not that Miss Polly held *that* against him—she had a lot of respect for the men who'd fought for this great country. But instead of getting a prosthesis fitted like most sensible folks would, he hopped around like a one-legged jackrabbit. "If'n the good Lord wanted me to git a new leg, he wouldn't a took the one Ah had," he'd say whenever anyone asked why he didn't get an artificial limb. No one argued with his reasoning, not when the Lord was involved.

As for the rest of Stumpville's male population, the only other romantic candidates were some teenaged boys whose mamas Miss Polly had known since they'd popped out of the womb—and she didn't want to go robbing the cradle! Everybody else was married or—like Sheriff Grizzle—

separated. (And he drank too much for Miss Polly's liking.) Now Mayor Calhoun wasn't too sorry a sight in the feller department. Problem was, he'd been married to the same woman since he'd finished high school—and part of that was her own dumb fault, since she hadn't taken his interest in her seriously, dismissing it as puppy love. So things didn't look too promising in the romance department for Polly DuKane.

But things looked promising for her elsewhere as the news media continued to descend on Stumpville, Georgia. Miss Polly displayed a natural ease on camera as if she'd been born to it. Not surprisingly, her oft-repeated tale of her brush with danger became increasingly embroidered with regard to the rather unusual dining patron she'd served fried chicken to on the day the bank next door had been robbed. "Ah was plumb terrified!" she cried, apparently forgetting her initial statements to the press about the individual seeming like "a nice lil' feller." Thanks to the waitress, A Taste of Heaven's hungry customer had now become the dwarf-demon spawn of Satan. "Ah kin always tell when somebody's got evil inside him. The eyes c'aint lie. They're the window to the soul!"

The press gobbled it up faster than the fried chicken Miss Polly served the diner's customers, though not for the reasons she believed. The small-town reporters simply found her an amusing character, like that embarrassing aunt everyone loved despite her social blunders. As for the big-city reporters and television news people, Polly DuKane was a reality TV series in the making.

Chapter Thirteen

THE "ANIMAL DWARF BANDITS" story had attracted the attention of every major news media outlet in the state, with the nationals reporting on it as well. Nate had even seen a segment on *Entertainment Tonight*. His pa had had a field day with that one, howling with laughter as Nate's eyes blurred with frustrated tears as he felt his story slipping farther and farther away.

"Ain't them those midgets y'all been writin' about for your newspaper?" cried Earl, pounding his fist on the battered arm of his recliner.

Nate didn't answer. Instead he sat on the sofa alongside his ma, wishing he was dead. At least being dead wouldn't hurt so bad.

But Earl Jessop wasn't the only one doing the laughing. Even TV newscasters couldn't keep a straight face as they reported on the dangerous gang of little people wearing animal masks and carrying Tommy Guns. Frequent reference was made to John Dillinger. Nate had to look him up on the Internet, since he'd never heard of the notorious gangster who'd robbed banks during the Great Depression. This Dillinger feller looked like he'd been a real bad apple too, which made the lack of seriousness with which the story was being covered even more surprising. Nate wouldn't get away with that kind of reporting at the *Pinewood Times-Courier*. Old man Clemson would've tied him to a fence and used him for target practice!

It was hopeless. Nate would never be able to compete with these big-time newspaper and TV reporters, not as long as he was stuck working for some rinky-dink small-town weekly in Shitsville, Georgia. So maybe the paper got read by a few folks in the county, but if you added everyone up together the circulation still didn't amount to spit. Nate's big journalism job was nothing but a dead-end. Even if he got lucky enough to one day take over as publisher and editor-in-chief the job would be a dead end. Anyways, Miss Mandy had a better chance than he did since she was related to the boss, blood being thicker than water. Old man Clemson wasn't going to hand over the reins to Nate when he retired what with his niece working there, not when she had a kid to support.

Nate had blown his chances at getting the scoop when he'd lost the trail of that little feller with the hat. Now he had no hope of being anything more than a parrot, repeating what everyone else said, then sticking his "Nate Jessop, Staff Reporter" by-line underneath it. That might be good enough for the *Pinewood Times-Courier*, but it wasn't good enough for Nate. Maybe it was time to call it quits. If he begged hard enough, Joe from the hardware store might give him his old job back or even promote him to manager if he worked there long enough. Of course his pa would never let him live it down, but at least Nate could get away from Miss Mandy before he did something stupid and ended up like his sister's boyfriend. Nate often wondered why Chester hung around, especially when he wasn't even married to Kimmie-Mae. Most guys would've taken off a long time ago. Nate didn't think Chester stayed out of love—he was too cynical to believe that. Seeing how his folks were with each other, how could he *not* be cynical?

As for Miss Mandy, she was becoming a real concern. Lately she'd been going around telling everybody how she wouldn't mind having another kid, dropping hints that she had her eye on Nate as the father. She was even talking about "settling down" and getting a home of her own—a *family* home to raise her kids in and take care of her husband. The morning Nate had walked past her desk and seen an open Web page on her PC screen for a site selling wedding dresses he knew he was a marked man.

So he began to rehearse in his head what he'd say so he didn't look like a complete loser when he quit his job. Everyone in town had seen him running from school to work to home almost every day of the week until he'd finally finished his college course and been handed his journalism certificate. That had been the proudest moment of his life. Nate had even put the certificate in a fancy gold frame. It now hung on the wall of his bedroom near the cross that had been there ever since he was born. His pa wouldn't let him hang it in the living room. Instead he acted like his son's achievement was something to be ashamed of. To think it'd all been for nothing! Nate had never felt so down in his life.

And then he saw it again—the little car with the Confederate flag on the roof.

Chapter Fourteen

IF THELONIOUS HADN'T STOPPED at a minimart to buy petrol and a cold drink, he might not have even noticed it. Until now the red pickup had been maintaining a sensible distance, but Thelonious's impromptu stop had caused it to close the gap. Rather than continuing on its way, the truck pulled over, waiting with the engine running until Thelonious had finished and driven off, at which point it fell smoothly into place behind him.

As he focused on the image in his rear-view mirror, Thelonious's neck tingled with an ursine warning. Surely this couldn't be the same clapped-out banger that had sent him running to that useless sheriff for help? Although Grizzle had been spot on when he'd said that just about everyone in the county drove a red pickup, Thelonious had a bad feeling about this. The way in which the truck's front bumper hung lower on one side like a menacing grin was too familiar.

Maybe he was overreacting. The driver might simply be going about his normal business, using the road the same as everyone else. Except no one else was using the road. Thelonious hadn't seen another vehicle since he'd left the minimart—and that was now several miles behind him. He had no idea where he even was. The hourglass on the SATNAV screen kept spinning round and round, which was how Thelonious's brain felt as he wavered between paranoia and panic. He checked his phone; not a bar showed on the display. It was as if he'd driven into a dead zone.

Thelonious slowed down, hoping the truck would overtake him and put his concerns to rest. Instead it slowed down right along with him, maintaining the same cautious distance. He waited a few minutes before dropping his speed still further. The pickup did the same, reducing its speed to such a degree that a pensioner with two broken legs could've outpaced it. Thelonious was now certain it had to be the same truck.

"Here we go again," he grumbled, his unease rapidly being replaced by anger. Just who did this banjo-plucking hillbilly think he was? Shaking his paw at the rear-view mirror, Thelonious let loose with a series of vivid expletives, none of which could be heard by the pickup's driver. He needed to get shot of this character once and for all. In fact, he needed to get shot of Pinewood County. The place was a breeding ground for loonies!

The trees lining the roadside merged into a greenish-brown blur as Thelonious flew past, his furry features rigid with determination. A laboured wheeze of sudden acceleration prompted him to take a curve too fast, the Mini's tyres kicking up dirt and stones as they skirted the shoulder. Although he constantly checked his mirrors, he couldn't see anything behind him but Georgia heat shimmering off an empty road. Rather than ease up on the accelerator, Thelonious urged the little car to go faster, the grinding of engine gears resonating in his ears like a death knell. Just because he couldn't see the pickup truck didn't mean it wasn't back there *somewhere.*

The gently rolling landscape became more forested as hardwoods competed for space with pines. The road went on and on, seeming to lead Thelonious away from civilisation rather than toward it. Then he saw a mailbox. Where there were mailboxes there must surely be houses. Perhaps if he pulled into one of their driveways and stayed out of sight, he could wait until the coast was clear. By the time the other driver realised he'd been hoodwinked, Thelonious would be back on the road heading in the opposite direction.

Thelonious swung into the next driveway he came to, nearly taking down the mailbox. The thing looked as if it had been beaten with a baseball bat. Its metal flap hung from one hinge, revealing an interior stuffed with what must've been several days' worth of mail. Adjacent to the mailbox was a newspaper holder with *Pinewood Times-Courier* stencilled on its side; a newspaper was still inside. Thelonious concluded that whoever lived here was very likely away.

The Mini bounced down the potholed driveway. Thelonious flinched as gravel pinged into the chassis, now regretting that he hadn't chosen a different driveway—preferably one that was paved. Suddenly he saw a small car parked next to a haphazard stack of firewood. At first he thought it was a Mini Cooper, but as he got closer he realised it was one of those foreign clones. Hopefully its owner was a long way from here. Having already survived one run-in for trespassing, Thelonious didn't think his luck would hold to survive another. He hadn't planned to come this far back, but the driveway was narrow and flanked by trees—he couldn't have turned around if he'd wanted to.

The log cabin blended so well with the wooded surroundings that Thelonious almost didn't see it. Its metal roof contained more dents than the mailbox, which wasn't surprising considering the number of trees leaning precariously toward it. The roof was also littered with pine needles and small branches, one of which had fallen across the chimney. Something had been eating away at the bottom row of logs on the cabin's exterior, the likely culprits being the insects swarming around the foundation. A scrubby front garden featured an uncoiled hose and a corroded weathervane with an ornamental rooster. Sagging wooden steps led to a sagging front porch and a pine front door with a window inset; its glass was cracked. The porch had been furnished with four low stools arranged around an old barrel. A dirty coffee mug sat forgotten on top along with a large can of bug spray.

Thelonious cut the engine. Since he hadn't seen any movement at the windows or door, he reckoned he'd be safe. Unbuckling his seatbelt, he pivoted around to watch the road. Within moments the labouring rattle of an engine reached his ears as a red pickup went past. He timed himself by the dashboard clock until five minutes had gone by. Any longer and he ran the risk of the driver realising his mistake and turning back. If the truck came down this driveway, Thelonious would be trapped. Plus he was beginning to have doubts about the cabin being empty—he thought he'd just seen the curtains twitching at one of the windows.

The parked car and the stack of firewood didn't leave the Mini with enough space to turn around. Thelonious had no choice but to reverse all the way up the driveway—and he very nearly took a couple of pine trees with him. This time he succeeded in knocking over the mailbox. It went clanging into the road, where it was flattened by a passing propane truck. Steering around the casualty, he drove back in the direction he'd come from. He remembered seeing a T-junction marked with state route numbers by the minimart. With any luck, one of the roads went north.

Which was how Thelonious ended up in the mountains several days earlier than planned.

Chapter Fifteen

NATE DROVE UP AND DOWN the same stretch of road three times, passing the same squashed mailbox. The little car with the Confederate flag had vanished.

"Dang it!" he shouted, bashing his fist against the steering wheel. That goldurn bank bandit could be halfway to Alabama by now! He knew he shouldn't have hung so far back, but he'd been worried about being too obvious, especially when the car kept slowing down, like its driver was testing him or something. Now he understood what made some folks crazy enough to go off shooting other folks—folks they didn't even know. Hopelessness. It was the worst feeling in the world—and Nate was feeling it big time.

Nate began to pray. He prayed for himself. He prayed for his ma. He even prayed for his pa, though that prayer was short because suddenly he had an idea. What if that feller had gone down one of the driveways? That could mean he was living around here. And if he lived around here, his partners in crime might too. Heck, the whole gang could be holed up in these woods, hiding out from the law. Folks in these parts were big on privacy, which was why so many houses and trailers were set way back from the road, sometimes behind gates or barriers. Half the time you couldn't even see them from all the trees. Bank robbers needed privacy to plan their heists and count their loot, especially bank robbers who didn't look like regular folks. While Nate had been chasing all over the place like a headless chicken, that bear feller was probably sitting with his feet up, drinking a beer like his pa. He had to find him!

But Nate knew he couldn't do it all on his own. For one thing, he risked getting his head blown off if he went snooping around on private property. Pretty much everyone had guns—and they weren't afraid to use them either. Plus there were enough meth labs in these woods to keep even the county tax assessor away. Nate needed help—*official* help— and he knew just where to get it.

When he saw Sheriff Grizzle's patrol car in the parking lot, Nate let out a whoop of pure joy. It had taken forever to drive back to Stumpville in his old truck, which seemed to be getting worse by the day with its groaning and wheezing and rattling. Nate had been worried the sheriff might be gone— he hadn't been able to get a signal to call and by the time he'd been in range of one, the charge on his crummy phone had died. He knew that once Sheriff Grizzle heard his theory, the two of them could team up on the case, with Nate acting as a sort of unofficial consultant. That way he'd be in on the action before the competition smelled it in the air. He also had another reason for wanting to speak to the sheriff—he was dying to know why the driver of the little car had been at the sheriff's department that other time Nate had been following him. Maybe the feller had been trying to cut a deal, like informing on his fellow bank robbers in return for a reduced or suspended sentence for his part in the robberies. Criminals did that all the time—or at least they did in the movies and on those TV shows.

"Sheriff Grizzle!" cried Nate, tripping over his own feet in his rush to get through the door. He could see the sheriff was about to leave; another minute and he'd have missed him completely.

If not for the fresh batch of apple fritters Miss Sue-Ann had brought in for the swing shift, Sheriff Grizzle would've been long gone. But he couldn't leave without eating at least two, chasing them down with a cup of coffee he'd added a secret splash of bourbon to. He'd just come out of the men's room when young Jessop came charging through the door like a bull in heat. Although the sheriff had nothing against the boy and didn't mind getting his picture in the paper if it showed him in a good light, he'd put in his hours for the day. All he wanted was to go home, sit on the front porch and make quick work of those cans of Bud waiting for him in the refrigerator. He might even get in some hunting before it got dark. He didn't much care what he shot—he just felt like killing something.

Sheriff Grizzle's tongue chased a flake of tobacco that had been hiding behind one of his back molars. When he finally caught it, he spat it out onto the linoleum floor, where it mingled with the faded pattern and all the other bits of tobacco he'd deposited there over the course of a day. "As y'all kin see, Ah's fixin' to go home!" he snapped at Nate. After that phone call this afternoon from his estranged wife asking for money (*again*), the sheriff had no patience left for anyone.

Despite the cool air blowing through the air-conditioning ducts, Nate felt his armpits dripping with sweat. It ran down his sides. He could even feel it in the crack of his butt and it was all he could do to stop himself from scratching back there. He sure hoped he didn't stink because if he did, Sheriff Grizzle would be in an even bigger hurry to get away. "Sheriff, I think I have a lead on one of those bank robbers!"

"How's that?"

"The bank robbers—I think I know where one of them

might be hiding out!"

The sheriff's roughhewn features became more attentive. "Y'all mean them midgets goin' around shootin' up banks?"

Nate nodded his head vigorously. "You got it, Sheriff!"

Clapping his hand on the younger man's shoulder, Sheriff Grizzle offered Nate a tobacco-stained smile. "Now listen here, son. Y'all need to be leavin' the police work to us law enforcement professionals. That's what we's here for!"

"Of course, Sheriff. It's just that—"

"Now Ah realise y'all's a newspaper reporter and jus' doin' your job. But Ah wouldn't be doin' *my* job if'n Ah let innocent folks git hurt helpin' us catch dangerous criminals."

Nate was practically hopping from foot to foot with excitement—he had to get Sheriff Grizzle to listen to him! "But that's just it, Sheriff. I saw one of the bank robbers not even an hour ago—and he was right here with you the other day too!" It was more like two hours ago when Nate had seen him, but the sheriff didn't need to know that.

"*Here?* With *me?*"

"Yes! You know—he drives that car with the Confederate flag on the roof. Remember?" Nate tried to hide his frustration. Sometimes the sheriff's memory wasn't too good. It was probably from all the drinking.

"Y'all mean that peculiar l'il bear feller?"

"That's the one!"

"Other'n bein' peculiar, he ain't done nothin' wrong far's Ah kin see. Though he kin sure use some drivin' lessons. Either that or a pair of eyeglasses. Plumb near crashed into Miss Sue-Ann's SUV!" The sheriff shook his large square head. "He sure got a lively imagination on him, Ah'll say that much. Seems like every time Ah see him he's got somethin' bitin' his bee-hind. Came runnin' on in here the other day with the craziest doggone story—"

One of the female office staff chose that moment to interrupt. "Here's that file y'all asked for, Sheriff," she said, handing him a thick manila folder.

Wedging it in his armpit, Sheriff Grizzle took it with him

to the coffeemaker and poured himself another cup. Grabbing the last apple fritter out of the basket, he swallowed it down in two bites, flicking away some crumbs that had landed on his shirtfront. He wandered over to the plate-glass window, where he stood staring out at the parking lot.

Nate kept following the sheriff around the office, feeling like an unwanted puppy. "I tried to see what he was up to," he continued. "But I lost him on highway twenty-two going east."

The sheriff turned to face him. "Y'all still worried about them midget bank bandits? Son, they's long gone by now. They'd be plumb crazy to stick around Pinewood County, trust me."

"Please, Sheriff Grizzle, just hear me out!" Before the sheriff could put him off again, Nate launched into his theory about the robbers living in one of the homes off the highway, becoming more inspired with each word. "They might even be hiding out in somebody's house!" he added.

Suddenly the sheriff perked up. "Y'all mean like a hostage situation?"

"Yes!" cried Nate. Getting the scoop on a story like that could really put him in the big leagues. "I mean, anything's possible!" To his surprise, Nate actually found himself hoping the dwarf bandits *had* taken a houseful of people hostage. Then he felt ashamed of himself. He wasn't being very Christian-like.

"Hmm…. It's definitely worth considerin'. How's about y'all lemme look into this?"

"Sure thing, Sheriff! What do you need me to do? I want to help in any way I can. And"—Nate hoped he wasn't pushing his luck—"maybe you can be my exclusive source on the case?"

Had he been too subtle? Sheriff Grizzle wasn't exactly the sharpest knife in the drawer as his ma liked to say. But Nate didn't want the sheriff talking to other reporters, especially when *he* was the one providing the leads. As he was about to rephrase his request, the sheriff steered him toward the exit.

"Y'all keep up the good work, son. And keep me posted on any dee-velopments."

"You bet!" said Nate, his face beaming. "And thanks so much for giving me this opportunity! It means a lot to me!"

But Sheriff Grizzle was no longer listening. In his mind he was sitting on his front porch with a can of beer and his hunting rifle, watching the sun disappearing behind the treetops.

The following morning the sheriff was back in his office chewing over what little he could recall of his conversation with young Nate Jessop. His head throbbed something awful. He'd drunk an entire six-pack of Bud after he'd gone home yesterday, chasing it with a third of a bottle of his favourite Kentucky bourbon. By the time he'd fetched his rifle out of the closet to do some hunting, he felt so woozy he keeled over backward onto the sofa, sleeping clear through to morning. Even a cold shower didn't do much to clear his head, but at least he didn't stink of liquor.

Another cup of coffee and it was starting to come back to him, including the fact that he'd been in Florida trying to make his wife see sense when he should've been here in Pinewood County taking care of business—business that now included a bank robbery at Stumpville Bank and Trust. He hadn't even learned about it until Sunday afternoon after he'd finished his moonlighting job controlling traffic for the American Church of God Ministry. Guess he got what he deserved for not checking in all weekend. Though it wasn't like his second-in-command had gone out of his way to find him either.

Although he'd been humouring young Nate to get rid of him, Sheriff Grizzle wondered if the boy might be on to something. Could it be he'd had one of them vicious bank-robbing midgets right here in front of him, only to let him go? Because it wasn't only once, but *three* times that bear feller had been in his face. That cockamamie yarn about a red pickup truck could've been a trick, something to throw him off the scent. Well, it wasn't going to work. Maynard Grizzle might not be some big-city police detective, but he wasn't some country hick either!

Sheriff Grizzle was ready for business. First up on the agenda—issue a "Be On The Lookout" advisory for the vehicle that flea-bitten critter had been driving. He might not have the make, model, licence plate number or name of the driver, but he did have *one* important detail for his BOLO: the car had a big ol' Confederate flag painted on the roof!

Chapter Sixteen

AS SOON AS THELONIOUS turned onto the highway leading to
the mountains, his muzzle began to twitch with an ancestral
memory. Cool mountain air carried scents of pine and grassy
meadows, along with the more distant scents of river water
and trout. He needed the kind of sanity that only nature could
provide. He needed to feel like a bear again.

The highway eventually linked up with a town that went
by the bucolic name of Dogwood Falls, though from what
Thelonious could see, there wasn't anything much bucolic
about it. Entering the town limits, he found himself
welcomed by a plethora of ESCAPE TO THE NORTH GEORGIA
MOUNTAINS! billboards flogging log cabins and mountain
homes to city escapees. He drove past several estate agents
before coming to a traffic light at a busy intersection. Here
more estate agents competed for space with a Baptist church,
a waffle restaurant, a fried chicken chain, a barbecue shack, a

bank, a thrift shop and a motor lodge.

Thelonious couldn't take another night of rattling ice machines and slamming doors and wailing kiddies. He wanted to live off the land for a bit—something he'd not done since his halcyon days as a cub. He remembered summer outings with his father in the woodland near their home, where they'd spend the day gorging themselves on wild berries, then snoozing in the sunshine until it was time to go home. Alas, such simple pleasures were short-lived due to the land being sold off to developers. They cut down the trees, replacing them with cookie-cutter housing estates and a giant Costco.

At the next traffic light Thelonious pulled into a service station. As he stood on his stepladder filling the Mini's tank, his gaze took in the unremarkable collection of shops across the highway. The "Dogwood Falls Shopping Center" housed an insurance agent's, a discount dollar shop, a dry cleaner's and a submarine sandwich chain he'd made a conscious decision to avoid since he didn't trust the artificial colour of their meat. There was also a freestanding bank with a drive-thru window. The "anchor" stores consisted of a sporting goods emporium and a supermarket with an overweight cartoon pig as its logo. Thelonious wasn't sure what sort of message this sent out to customers, but judging from the stream of people going inside to buy groceries, it didn't seem to be putting anyone off.

Big Al's Sporting Goods utilised a more direct marketing approach with its SALE! sign plastered across the front window. It looked as if it had been there for some time, having gone tattered at the edges. Thelonious wondered if "Big Al" existed or if this was one of those folksy American names invented by men in suits as a way to convince shoppers they'd get the quality, service and prices of small-town yesteryear. To their credit, the Yanks were far better at selling goods—especially goods no one really needed—than the Brits. Suddenly he realised that everything for his mountain adventure was right here in front of him.

Thelonious parked next to an SUV with a Florida licence plate and an I FEAR NO FISH! bumper sticker. Big Al's glass doors whooshed open at his approach. Canned country music greeted him along with the strong odour of tyre rubber, which originated from a display of mountain bikes that had their prices marked down. Thelonious toddled past the shopping trolleys with their impossible-to-reach handlebars, doing likewise with the handheld plastic carriers. He'd ask one of the sales staff to help him get everything up to the till and later, out to the car.

A teenaged lad with an acne condition manned the only open check-out counter—and he was too busy texting on his phone to bother with the likes of customers, especially customers located below eye level. Thelonious's polite "hello" as he passed went unacknowledged. The cashier seemed to be the only employee about—even the customer service counter had no one behind it. Fortunately there were enough signs directing shoppers to various categories of merchandise. Thelonious trundled determinedly toward CAMPING AND HIKING.

Although he eventually found everything he wanted, it had taken far longer than he'd expected. Almost all of the sale-priced goods had been placed too high up on the shelves, requiring Thelonious to climb onto any available object to reach them. Many items had been packed into bulky boxes. These he cradled in his short arms, nearly toppling over as he made his way toward checkout. What he couldn't carry he pushed, dragged or kicked across the floor, never once receiving any offers of assistance. As he waited for everything to be rung up, Thelonious noticed a framed photograph on the store's display wall. The face in the image matched that of the acne-plagued cashier. Beneath it was a bronze rectangle with the inscription EMPLOYEE OF THE YEAR.

Big Al's star employee loaded everything into a shopping trolley as if it were his goal to make it as unstable as possible, sending Thelonious on his way with a robotic "Thanks for shopping at Big Al's."

Thelonious blindly pushed the wonky contraption outside to the car park. The corner of a box coming through the plastic latticework kept poking him in the muzzle, though when he tried to turn away he almost lost an eye. A blast of a horn as he entered the pedestrian crossing zone nearly caused him to tip over the trolley. He'd barely cleared the area before the SUV with the fishing bumper sticker zoomed past.

Thelonious was now the owner of a one-person tent with zippered privacy flap, a fleece sleeping bag, a camping pillow, a folding canvas chair, an oil lantern, a three-piece "mess" kit for cooking and boiling water, a small barbecue grill, a bag of charcoal, a bottle of lighter fluid, matches, a fly-fishing rod-and-reel combo with line, and an assortment of plastic trout lures. Although he hadn't gone fly fishing since he was a cub, Thelonious reckoned it was like riding a horse—once you got in the saddle, it all came back. Or was that a bike? Not that he'd ridden a horse or a bike before….

The supermarket with its cartoon pig mascot was next. Thelonious tottered up and down the aisles with a carrier basket on each arm. He only planned to get a few essentials since he'd be dining on trout fresh from the river. Once again much of what he wanted had been placed beyond his reach. Usually he avoided such inconveniences by ordering his groceries online, but now he found his voice creaking with embarrassment as he asked other shoppers and store employees for assistance. Unlike Big Al's, the staff actually cared about customer service; the shoppers had been nice too. An old codger in a motorised wheelchair even offered Thelonious the use of his lap.

"Why'nt y'all hop on up here and let me drive?" he invited, patting thin thighs that couldn't support the weight of a sparrow.

Thelonious graciously declined, though he couldn't keep from grinning at the comical image of himself whizzing up and down the aisles standing on the old man's lap.

Bread, peanut butter, granola bars, peaches, sugar, tea bags, powdered creamer and a can of no-stick cooking spray went into one basket. To this Thelonious added paper plates, disposable cups, plastic cutlery, a small bottle of eco-friendly washing-up liquid, a four-pack of loo roll, and a packet of wet wipes. The second basket held a supply of bottled water, its weight causing him to lurch sideways like a furry Quasimodo as he waddled toward the check-out aisles. He joined one of the queues, grunting as he set the heavy baskets onto the floor. Suddenly he heard giggling.

A trio of tots swarmed like flies around an angry-looking woman wearing a baggy tracksuit patterned with shiny flowers. Their shopping trolley overflowed with every boxed and junk food imaginable. The only item with any potential for nutrition seemed to be a breakfast cereal, though Thelonious revised his opinion when he saw that it contained coloured marshmallows. The children whined and fidgeted as their mother hurled groceries onto the conveyor belt with no regard for the cashier, who looked as if she needed a stiff drink. Thelonious's muzzle wrinkled in disgust as he detected the odour of a nappy in urgent need of changing. The air quality improved considerably after the family's departure, as did the cashier's spirits when it came time for Thelonious's purchases to be rung up. He even earned himself a "Y'all have a nice day!" when she leaned over to hand him his sales receipt, though she quickly pulled back when he gave her a toothy grin. Sometimes he forgot how intimidating his choppers could be.

Thelonious had enough provisions to see him through a few days. If the trout turned out to be as fat and plentiful as he anticipated, he wouldn't even need to leave his campsite, because his supermarket would be right outside his tent. He stopped off at the bank to replenish his supply of dollars, ignoring the staring eyes of customers and employees as he balanced on his stepladder in front of the ATM machine. "Take a picture, it lasts longer!" he growled, baring his teeth at no one in particular. Pretty soon he'd be in a place where the only staring eyes belonged to a trout.

Leaving Dogwood Falls, Thelonious continued to travel

north in search of his riverfront utopia, relieved when the estate agent billboards finally gave way to the occasional billboard offering kayaking adventures. His online searches had come up with a number of picturesque locations suitable for camping; hopefully they wouldn't be busy on a weekday. The last thing he wanted was to share his haven with a bunch of partying youths or families with screaming children. He might even do some hiking—the famous Appalachian Trail was up here somewhere. Perhaps he'd ask another hiker to take a few photos of him with the mountainous scenery in the background. He'd never been too chuffed with that "author portrait" on his book jacket. It made him look like a child's stuffed teddy bear.

Although he hadn't planned to make any more stops, Thelonious found the little country store hard to resist. The hand-lettered signs touting farm-fresh produce, cider, sorghum syrup, homemade jams and jellies, local honey and the ubiquitous boiled peanuts gave the place a down-home Southern feel that would fit nicely into his book. A tumbledown front porch offered up a variety of garden decorations to entice customers to part with their money. Thelonious saw planters, weathervanes, wind chimes, bird feeders and painted gourds. There were even some impressive wood carvings of bears that had been done with a chainsaw. After photographing the shack-like structure from different angles, he decided to go inside and have a look around.

Prying open the warped screen door, Thelonious's nostrils were instantly assailed by the smell of fruit going off. Cardboard boxes had been set out containing peaches, melons, tomatoes, potatoes, peppers, onions, green beans and cucumbers. Tiny flies circled overhead like microscopic planes waiting to land. Good thing he'd bought peaches at the supermarket, because the ones on offer here looked rotten or close to it. Thelonious went over to a display rack to peruse the modest selection of guidebooks on the Appalachian Trail, selecting one located toward the bottom, not realising until too late that it was coated with the same reddish dust that also coated the worn wooden floorboards. He wiped his paws discreetly on a Confederate flag sticking out of a metal bucket with others being sold as souvenirs of the American South.

"How y'all doin'?"

Startled, Thelonious turned around to see an old man seated at an ancient cash register. A box labelled MOON PIES and a jar of deer jerky were on the counter at his elbow. Unscrewing the lid, the shopkeeper helped himself to a piece of jerky, offering Thelonious a smile made unintentionally comical by the fact that it contained no front teeth, though their absence didn't stop him from fighting with the dried meat as he tried to gnaw off a manageable portion.

"Fine, thank you," replied Thelonious, hoping he hadn't been seen using the Confederate flag as a towel.

"Y'all lookin' for somethin' special?"

Thelonious nodded toward the front porch. "Did you do the bear carvings?"

"Nah. Them's done by a local feller—Jim Hardee. Big Jimbo, we call him." The old man stared hard at Thelonious, then grinned. "Ah kin see why y'all might be innerested. Seein' it's near closin' time, Ah kin give y'all a discount iff'n you're lookin' to buy."

Although Thelonious wasn't in the market for a chainsaw-carved bear, he couldn't help thinking that the purchase of one might make the proprietor more amenable to having his photograph taken. Although not keen on portraiture, Thelonious couldn't let this opportunity pass. The old man's face told the history of the American South. Thelonious saw hardship and toil, misery and joy. He saw a life lived decently despite the odds. "I might be," he said, wondering what he was going to do with a carved wooden bear.

An hour later Thelonious had several new images on his camera's memory card and a signed release granting permission to use them. He couldn't believe how easy it had been. The minute he'd learned that Thelonious was doing a photography book on the American South, the shopkeeper couldn't sign the consent form fast enough, his claim to be shutting for the day apparently forgotten. He didn't even pull a face when Thelonious dragged his folding stepladder inside so he could be at the correct height for portrait shots. After they'd finished, the old man kept him there for still another hour, bombarding him with questions.

"Darned shame y'all ain't got a wife," he said after Thelonious replied that he wasn't married. "Every feller should have hisself a wife. Heck, Ah had me two! 'Course one up and died on me so Ah had to git me another." He gave Thelonious a gap-toothed grin. "Wouldn't want y'all thinkin' Ah'm one of them—what they call them folks a'gin—*bigamosts*?"

"I think it's 'bigamist,'" corrected Thelonious, trying to hide his own grin.

"Whatever." The old man waved his hand dismissively. "If'n y'all lookin' for a nice gal, my grandbaby ain't hitched yet. Rayleen just turned nineteen, but don't let that put y'all off. She's still purdy as a picture!"

Thelonious's face reddened beneath his fur. "Thank you, but I'm not looking."

The shopkeeper's grin turned to a scowl. "Why's that?" he asked suspiciously. "Y'all one of them homosexuals?"

"No!"

"If'n y'all ask me, them folks just ain't normal. And don't let nobody tell y'all different neither!" The old man stuck his hand into the jar of jerky, coming out with another piece. "So y'all got kin in the area?"

"Actually, I'm from England."

"*England?* My brother-in-law went thare once! He didn't much like it though. Rained all the time. And if it wasn't rainin', the wind was blowin' folks to kingdom come! Food's plumb awful too."

"Sorry to hear that."

"Yep. He couldn't even git any grits or biscuits and gravy.

Kin y'all believe it? He couldn't git no sweet tea neither. Them English folks put milk in their tea." He grimaced. "Now that ain't right!"

Thelonious needed to be on his way if he ever hoped to find his nature idyll before dark. Plus the shopkeeper's nosy questions were exhausting. He reckoned the old man was bored or lonely. Maybe no one ever stopped here, especially if they wanted produce that hadn't passed its sell-by date. Thelonious was eventually rescued by a ringing telephone— the old man's missus calling to find out why her husband hadn't come home yet. The next thing Thelonious knew he was being ushered out the door with a carved wooden bear tucked beneath one arm and a jug of sorghum syrup tucked beneath the other, a guidebook on the Appalachian Trail stuck into the waistband of his trousers. A Moon Pie was stuffed into his mouth—a freebie from the old proprietor when he'd noticed Thelonious eyeing the display. The gooey amalgamation of marshmallow and cookie crumbs soon had him longing for a toothbrush. It didn't taste all that fresh either. He waited until he was out of sight before spitting it onto the ground. A horde of ants promptly attacked it, clearly having a greater appreciation of sweets with the flavour and texture of old bed linen.

The carved bear sat upright on the Mini's back seat; Thelonious thought it cruel to chuck it into the boot like a piece of luggage. It didn't occur to him that he'd assumed the role of chauffeur until later when he heard himself asking if his passenger might like to listen to some music. These twisting mountain roads were doing his head in—and the motorbikes flying past at warp speed weren't helping. Hopefully it wouldn't be too much longer.

Suddenly the distant scent of trout Thelonious had noticed earlier that day became more pronounced. As he rounded a bend, the trees on one side of the road thinned out, revealing a river. The late-afternoon sunlight sparkled on the bubbling water as it flowed over rocks and downed tree limbs. Thelonious roared with delight, raising a paw in victory. Then just as suddenly as it appeared the river disappeared as the road curved upward, leading him into dense woodland. A large Smokey the Bear sign greeted him with a stern warning about forest fires. Thelonious had now entered one of America's national forests. About a mile later he came to another much smaller sign; this one displayed the symbols for hiking and camping.

And river access.

Thelonious steered a hard right onto the marked byway, which immediately changed from asphalt to dirt. The Mini bounced downhill, the patchy road eventually levelling out as it ran parallel to the river. Although he'd expected to see at least *some* activity in a designated campground, there wasn't a vehicle or tent in sight. It was just nature and the river's soothing music. Thelonious parked beneath a tree by the riverbank, though he didn't get out straightaway. Instead he sat for a moment taking it all in, already feeling his blood pressure lowering. There'd be no rattling ice machines or slamming doors ruining his sleep tonight.

It was time to set up camp. Thelonious began by removing the wrappings from his purchases, frustrated by the ridiculous amounts of cardboard and plastic he had to get through. At this rate he'd have enough refuse to start his own landfill. He placed the barbeque grill in a small clearing along with the folding canvas chair, mess kit and bag of charcoal. The Mini's boot he converted into a makeshift bin since the only trash receptacle he could find had been bolted shut and had bear warnings posted all over it. Evidently some of his Southern brethren were capable of getting into a spot of mischief when the mood took them.

The "E-Z assembly" instructions that came with the tent had Thelonious snarling at anything that crossed his path, including a squirrel that had stopped by to investigate. Uttering a bark of protest, the creature scurried off to inform his cohorts about the ill-tempered bear who'd taken up residence in the neighbourhood. Soon more squirrels arrived, making themselves at home in the trees to watch the fun.

Thelonious could hear them chittering with laughter, which did little to improve his mood. He felt like setting fire to the tent, but he hated to let anything get the better of him, especially some cheap piece of rubbish made in China.

Although he eventually managed to get it assembled, Thelonious wasn't too impressed with the results. He knew he should've opted for a more expensive pop-up model, despite the fact it had seemed like a waste of money at the time. With any luck this budget version would see him through the next few days, provided a high wind didn't blow through the campsite. Thelonious furnished his new digs with the sleeping bag, pillow and oil lantern. The pair of pyjamas he'd unpacked from his suitcase he placed on his "bed." While prancing pink and blue bunnies weren't his first choice in sleepwear, he didn't have many fashion options when shopping in children's departments. The Appalachian Trail guidebook he left by the lantern, since he planned to do a bit of reading before bedtime. Despite the synthetic smell, the tent was surprisingly cosy.

Thelonious considered changing into his swimming trunks and taking a refreshing dip in the river. Other than the packet of wet wipes, the river would be his sole source for washing while he was here. But the lovely dappled pattern of the sunlight on the water instead had him toddling over with his camera. He even managed to photograph some trout leaping playfully into the air. They actually seemed to invite him to reach out and catch them with his bare paws. Thelonious wondered if he had it in him. His ancestors and woodland contemporaries wouldn't use a contraption invented by humans to do the job—they'd grab what they wanted and be done with it. When the playfulness became more like taunting, he decided he'd had enough. It was time to get cracking with a tasty seafood dinner!

The rod-and-reel combo felt clumsy in Thelonious's paws as he teetered at the river's edge, trying not to fall in. Worse still, the lures looked exactly like what they were—moulded bits of coloured plastic designed to fool trout into believing they were food. Although the artificial bait had looked real enough in the sporting goods store, in practice they were a sorry substitute for what could be found in nature. Thelonious cast the rod again and again until his shoulder hurt. The insects dive-bombing him grew bolder, swarming around his head and crawling into his eyes and nostrils. He saw his fishy opponents in the river gobble them down as they hovered too close to the water's surface. With such tasty chow on offer, why would they dine on plastic? The trout leapt into the air in defiance before scuttling down the river with their prey, their glassy eyes full of mirth as Thelonious carried on with his feeble attempts to catch his dinner. The shadowy campsite got darker as the sun disappeared behind a mountain. Soon there wouldn't be any light left to see by.

Abandoning his fishing gear on the bank, Thelonious stomped back to the tent. Grabbing one of the plastic supermarket bags he'd left inside, he took it with him to the canvas chair, sitting down to what would now be his dinner. He chewed morosely on a peach that had looked ripe but wasn't, interspersing it with hunks of bread the texture of moist clay, washing everything down with the sorghum syrup since he had no other use for it. It was like a poor man's version of maple syrup, with a rather bitter taste that perfectly suited his mood. Thelonious stared morosely at the barbeque grill, which remained as pristine as when he'd first unpacked it from the box. He felt like kicking it into the river.

As dusk draped itself over the little campsite, he became aware of woodland creatures moving about. When he spied a family of deer nibbling at the vegetation on the far side of the river, his spirits soared. The two little ones trailed after their mother, who constantly checked behind her to make sure they were close by. Thelonious thought he saw a buck farther back in the woods, but the dwindling light made it difficult to tell. The trio appeared to be enjoying their dinner, which must've been *haute cuisine* compared to the processed bread and unripe peach he'd just forced down his gullet.

Suddenly Thelonious heard gunshots. The deer family

bolted into the woods. Not wanting to put himself in harm's way, he followed suit, scrambling into his tent and zipping the flap closed. The shots sounded again, this time closer. He ducked his head instinctively, though no bullets passed through the nylon fabric. Thelonious's fear quickly turned to fury. How dare his peaceful evening by the river be ruined by some hunters? Surely it couldn't be legal to hunt near a public campground. Though who could he report it to, Smokey the Bear?

The gunshots grew fainter, eventually stopping altogether. Nevertheless, Thelonious stayed put. He leafed through his guidebook until the last of the light was gone. An entire chapter was devoted to murders that had taken place on the Appalachian Trail, some still unsolved. He flung the book into a corner. The tree limbs created sinister silhouettes against the tent, though it was pitch-black inside. Thelonious couldn't even see his paw in front of his face, yet he wouldn't risk lighting the oil lantern in case someone might still be out there. Instead he spent a restless night cowering in his sleeping bag, trying to ignore a pressing need for a wee. But he didn't dare stick his muzzle outside the tent. Especially when the noises began....

At first it was a scuffling. Thelonious immediately feared that the hunters had wandered into his campsite looking for prey or worse, looking for *another* kind of prey. Campers would be easy targets for criminals or psychopaths, particularly unarmed campers like Thelonious. Not only could they steal his money and credit cards, they could steal his camera gear and his car. They could even kill him. How utterly daft it had been to go camping, especially in a deserted campsite. He could vanish off the face of the earth and no one would know. He wouldn't even be missed except maybe by his publisher—and that would only be because he'd been paid half his advance on a book that would never be delivered.

The scuffling gave way to a plodding, like someone with a clumsy gait. It circled the tent, at times close enough to cause the fabric to ripple. Thelonious couldn't tell if it was one set of footsteps he heard or two—and he didn't intend to unzip the flap to find out. Whoever it was didn't seem to be going away any time soon.

"Hello?" he croaked.

No point in pretending he wasn't here—a tent in a public campground was about as subtle as one of Pastor Jehoshaphat Jones's billboards. The noises stopped, only to be replaced by heavy breathing.

"I've got a gun!" he cried, his growly voice sounding feeble even to his own ears.

His muzzle twitched with a faint recognition as the tent's mesh ventilation panels delivered to his nostrils an odour. Although not necessarily offensive, it wasn't something he cared to smell all night either. As the heavy breathing continued, Thelonious shimmied deeper into his sleeping bag, leaving just the furry tips of his ears exposed. His hearing had gone to high alert, though he sensed that whoever was out there had begun to do some listening of his own.

Thelonious's wide staring eyes could see nothing but the inky blackness inside the tent. Although he was now certain his nocturnal caller was alone, he didn't put much faith in a waterproof sheet of nylon protecting him from some crazed mountain man or serial killer. He wished he'd bought a weapon—even a baseball bat would've come in handy. He was at just the right height to inflict a fair bit of damage to someone's knee caps. Suddenly Thelonious heard snuffling at the zippered flap of his tent. It was followed by a low growling. He wondered if he'd live through the night.

Then all went quiet other than the chirring of crickets and the sound of the river. At some point during the night Thelonious fell asleep because the next thing he knew morning light illuminated the tent's interior. He listened for any sounds of danger, but the plodding footfalls were gone, along with the snuffling and growling. Instead his ears were treated to the cheerful music of birds. Sitting up in his sleeping bag, Thelonious stretched his furry arms above his head and yawned, working up the courage to investigate what was happening outside his flimsy safety zone. Although he considered it unlikely that last night's caller was still lurking in the vicinity, he wasn't about to blindly leap from the tent in his bunny pyjamas, belting out a chorus of "Zip-a-Dee-Doo-Dah."

Unzipping the flap halfway, he peered out. Other than the feathered songsters and a pair of bickering squirrels, the campsite appeared to be empty. Squeezing his feet into his trainers, Thelonious grabbed a roll of loo paper and the packet of wet wipes from a grocery bag and ventured out into the cool mountain morning, almost stepping in a mound of bear poo that had been left at the entrance to his tent.

It was still steaming.

Thelonious had barely completed his private business behind a tree than he was tossing everything back into the Mini. Although he checked up and down the riverbank, his new fishing rod was nowhere to be seen. Unless the family of deer or his visitor with the disgraceful toilet etiquette had decided to take up fly fishing, the culprits had to be the hunters. Even the bag of charcoal was gone, though the barbeque grill hadn't been touched. He wondered if Big Al's would give him a refund.

Still dressed in his pyjamas, Thelonious drove away from the campground. He'd been in such a hurry to leave that he didn't notice the yellow and brown coil snoozing on the Mini's sun-warmed Union Jack. He switched on the stereo, upping the volume to drown out the echo of last night's gunshots. The next time he fancied a bit of nature, he'd watch a David Attenborough documentary on the telly.

The national forest eventually came to an end, surrendering to secluded cabins and the occasional trailer. Thelonious passed a youth hostel, then a shop-cum-café catering to the hiking and motorbike crowd. Even at this early hour of the morning the car park was filled with motorbikes as well as hikers with heavy backpacks loitering in the vicinity of the portable toilets. When Thelonious saw the turn-off for a town, he took it. He wanted a clean motel room with a proper bathroom and a proper bed—and this time he didn't care what it cost.

With the music turned so loud, Thelonious didn't hear the siren until some time had passed—and by then the patrol car was so close on his tail he could smell what the driver had eaten for breakfast. He started to panic, not only weaving in his lane, but crossing into the oncoming one. The Mini's side and rear-view mirrors showed the officer sticking his arm out the window, signalling for Thelonious to pull over. Thelonious veered onto the shoulder and stopped. The patrol car followed suit, pulling up close behind him.

Thelonious could feel the back of his head burning as he watched in the mirrors the driver of the patrol car watching *him* from behind a pair of sunglasses. It reminded him of those stand-off scenes in Western films, with everyone waiting to see which cowboy drew his gun first. Finally the officer stepped out of his vehicle. Planting his hands on his boxy hips, he stood there staring at Thelonious, who was now too terrified to move—especially after he caught sight of the size of the gun holstered to the man's hip. From what Thelonious had heard about American policing methods, he'd end up being shot before he'd even taken his next breath.

Whatever reason this copper had for pulling him over, it probably wasn't for driving in his pyjamas.

Chapter Seventeen

"SHUT OFF THAT ENGINE RIGHT NOW!" Sheriff Vernon Purdue ordered the petrified-looking driver of the little car.

When he'd first seen the BOLO issued by Sheriff Maynard Grizzle, Vernon suspected his counterpart at the other end of the state had been visiting the meth labs in his county for more than just his regular monthly pay-off. Either that or he was drinking too much of the local moonshine. Having worked with the sheriff a ways' back when they were both young deputies, he was leaning toward the moonshine. By now every law enforcement officer in Georgia had heard about the armed gang of bank-robbing dwarves wearing animal masks. But being told to be on the lookout for an actual *bear* driving a car with a Confederate flag on the roof? That was a stretch even for Grizzle! Anyway, wasn't it the chicken who'd been driving the getaway car?

Vernon had forgotten all about it until a vehicle matching

the description given in the BOLO showed up on the highway smack dab in front of his patrol car. Usually he wouldn't have given such a crazy story the time of day (even if it *did* come from a fellow sheriff), but the God-fearing folks in these mountains relied on him to keep them safe—and Sheriff Purdue took that responsibility very seriously. He considered looking after his neighbours as the Lord's work and felt blessed that the county paid him a nice salary to do it. If one of those pint-sized robbers stepped foot in one of his local banks to steal his neighbours' hard-earned money, Vernon Purdue would make him regret being born.

Hitting the lights and siren, the sheriff put the pedal to the metal until he was nose to tail with the other vehicle. He couldn't for the life of him see who was driving. All he saw was a hat—and it was on the passenger side. The car definitely had a flag painted on the roof; it was red, white and blue with crisscrossing stripes. Although Vernon couldn't swear on the Bible it was Confederate, it sure looked like it. His first priority was to get the vehicle off the road before the driver caused an accident. It wasn't unusual for folks to get scared when they saw a police car behind them. Being scared wasn't the same thing as being guilty, though weaving all over the place could be a sign that the driver had had a few too many before getting behind the wheel. Alcohol abuse was a big problem in these parts. Some folks liked to get an early start to the day, drinking their breakfasts instead of eating them. He'd do a breathalyser test on the driver just to make sure.

The old-timers were the worst. Sheriff Purdue had seen more than his fair share of accidents from a routine traffic stop gone wrong, ending in a wreck or even a heart attack. Some of the deputies got a thrill out of folks soiling their pants and actually went out of their way to create a situation, but not Vernon. He'd been brought up better than that. He went to church every Sunday, thanked the Lord for every meal, and worked hard to support his family. He didn't have some fancy education or fancy college degree. High school had been it for him, along with his law-enforcement training. Anything outside of that he didn't need to know.

The sheriff loved these mountains. He loved being able to afford a big house on several acres of land—somewhere nice for his son and daughter to grow up and eventually, for him and his wife to grow old. Life was perfect here. Which was why he wished them city folks from Atlanta and those goldang Floridians would stay the heck away instead of clogging up the highways on weekends and buying houses they only spent a few days a year in. Although he had nothing against their money helping the local economy, it would be better if things went back to how they used to be when everybody knew their neighbours and the names of their young'uns and grandbabies.

But Vernon knew he was fighting a losing battle. You couldn't keep paradise a secret forever, especially when you had those real estate folks fighting over the same pie. Good Christians or not, they'd sell to *anyone*. Even the homosexuals were moving in. Vernon didn't approve of Sodomites and he knew the Lord didn't either—it said so in the Scripture. Just last weekend he'd seen some of them lesbian women shopping at Walmart, and he was sure he'd seen one in the paint section at Home Depot too. They all worshipped at that Unitarian Universalist Church—which everybody knew wasn't a real church at all! Next thing it'll be the blacks coming in. Not that the sheriff was racist or homophobic, but some folks needed to stay where they belonged—with their *own* kind.

As for the little car with the flag on the roof, it wasn't from anywhere around here. Sheriff Purdue had seen these foreign Mini cars before and he didn't like them. If it wasn't made in America, he had no use for it. Ford and Chevy were the only dealerships in these mountains and the locals wouldn't have it any other way. Americans needed to be spending their money on American-made products, not be making other countries rich. Vernon and his father and his father before him had fought in wars to keep this great country free. They had *not* fought in wars to fill the pockets of a bunch of rice-eating communists.

When the Mini Cooper pulled over, Sheriff Purdue was right behind it. Cutting the siren but leaving the lights, he entered the vehicle's licence plate number into the patrol car's mobile computer. As he waited to see if anything came back, he noticed something moving on the roof of the car. It looked like a snake. The computer returned no information—not that he'd expected it to since the car had a foreign plate and Vernon only had access to state and federal searches.

Unfolding his bulky frame from behind the steering wheel, he stood for a moment assessing the situation and more so, to catch his breath. He knew he should be watching his weight, but his wife made the best fried chicken and biscuits in the South *and* the best pecan pie. The Mini's engine was still running, which put the sheriff on red alert. He strode over to the driver's-side window, his hand within quick reach of his holstered firearm.

The seat was empty.

To Vernon's surprise, the steering wheel was on the wrong side of the vehicle—and seated behind it was a small bear wearing a hat. Looked like Maynard Grizzle had been sober after all.

In his most no-nonsense bark, Sheriff Purdue ordered the driver to turn off the engine. Only when this had been complied with did he cross to the other side of the car. The critter looked so terrified Vernon actually felt sorry for him. The driver was a bear all right. And not only that, he was wearing pyjamas!

A laminated card and a document of some kind were being thrust toward him. "Thelonious T. *Bear*?" he read aloud, wondering if this might be a gag. Although the card looked like a genuine driver's licence, Vernon had no idea what a genuine driver's licence from the United Kingdom even looked like. As for the photo, it matched the driver, minus the hat. The accompanying document seemed to be a vehicle registration, also UK-issued. He squinted at the driver, still not convinced. Some of his deputies had a weird sense of humour, though planning anything this crazy would take more brains than any of them had put together.

"Thelonious T. Bear," he repeated. "That you?"

"Yes." The growl at the end of the word didn't sit too well with the normally good-natured sheriff. Seemed he'd found himself one crabby little critter.

"Y'all aware you're drivin' with a rattlesnake on your vehicle?"

"A *rattlesnake?*" The driver's paws tightened on the steering wheel.

Nervous little critter too, mused Vernon, though he didn't get any sense of a threat. "Yep."

"Is it still there?"

"Yep. Though Ah think it's fixin' to leave." Sheriff Purdue watched as the snake slowly uncoiled itself and slid down the Mini's back window. Dropping to the dirt, it slithered off into the weeds. He wasn't a big fan of snakes, especially those that rattled.

"Is that why you stopped me?" The driver's rapid chuffing smelled to the sheriff like river water. Suddenly he had a hankering for some trout. Maybe he'd go fly fishing this weekend.

"No, it ain't." Vernon leaned in through the car window to see what was inside. Other than a small carrying case on the floor in front and some grocery bags on the floor in back, there wasn't anything worth noticing except a wooden bear, which sat on the back seat like a passenger. It was one of those chainsaw carvings popular with folks in the mountains—especially folks who weren't local. This one seemed to have something eating away at it. Vernon suspected woodworm. "That your mascot?" Receiving no answer, he continued. "So y'all from England?"

The hat nodded.

"Y'all sure a long way from home. What's your business in these parts?" Although he liked to give the impression of being all relaxed and casual-like, Sheriff Purdue never let down his guard. Despite crime being low in the mountains, the occasional incident cropped up that made him appreciate his weapons training. Luckily he and his deputies didn't need to use their guns very often. The expectation of force usually calmed even the most stubborn of characters—and a Taser provided extra convincing. But since the vehicle and its driver were such a close match for Sheriff Grizzle's BOLO, Vernon kept his hand by his holster, not wanting to take any chances in case this Thelonious T. Bear turned out to be one of the bank robbers.

"Work."

"Come ag'in?"

"I'm here for work!"

This Bear feller sure had a temper on him. Vernon was liking him less and less by the minute. "Thare ain't no call to git ornery," he admonished, his fingers inching closer to the butt of his firearm. "What kind of work y'all do then?"

As the driver began to loosen his grip on the steering wheel, Vernon tensed. "Y'all keep your hands where Ah kin see them!" he hollered, ready to draw his weapon. *Hands?* Maybe he should've said "paws."

Suddenly the sheriff wondered if he'd found himself an illegal alien. They had a few in the area, though they mostly came from places like Mexico and Central America. They worked in the fields, picking apples or whatever else needed picking. When they weren't doing that, they got hired as cheap labour on landscaping or construction jobs, taking less pay than an American would. Beau, Sheriff Purdue's brother-in-law, was always running off at the mouth about illegals stealing American jobs. Since his sister's husband was too lazy to get up off his fat behind to do anything that resembled work, Vernon couldn't see how some Mexican was stealing the food off the man's supper table.

And matching description or not, Vernon couldn't see how this sorry-looking critter from that pansy little island was out robbing banks either. Robbing a garbage bin for scraps of food, maybe. But banks? Maynard Grizzle must've been playing an April Fool's joke when he'd issued that BOLO.

Except it wasn't April.

Sheriff Purdue listened to the driver's explanation, though the gravelly voice and foreign accent were enough to try even the good Lord's patience. If he'd heard right, this Thelonious T. Bear was a photographer from London, England, and he'd travelled to Georgia to take pictures for a book. The next thing he knew the driver was reaching toward the carrying case on the floor. "Hold it right thare!" he shouted, whipping his gun out of its holster and aiming it at the critter's furry snout. Another stunt like that and Vernon would have him lying spread-eagled in the dirt.

"But I only wanted to show you some photos on my camera!"

Sheriff Purdue lowered his gun. A little. "Y'all take it nice and easy and put your hands—Ah mean your *paws*—right back on that steerin' wheel!" he ordered. Maybe he should just cuff the suspect and call for backup, though he doubted the cuffs would fit. Usually he had plastic cable ties, but he'd run out last week and kept forgetting to visit the supply room. Okay, he'd take a peek inside that carrying case and see what's what. If something didn't smell right, he'd bundle this Bear feller into the trunk of his patrol car and drive him to the station with sirens blaring!

"Now pass me that case real slow." As the driver unlocked his paws from the steering wheel, Vernon's gun hand twitched. "Keep one hand on the steerin' wheel!" he shouted. "This here gun's got a full clip—and Ah ain't got a problem with emptyin' it neither." Although the part about the gun was true, the emptying part was not. Sheriff Purdue hadn't shot anyone in the entire time he'd been with the sheriff's department.

The driver leaned slowly toward the carrying case, his short arm straining to reach the strap. After three attempts he finally managed to grab hold, pulling the case up onto the passenger seat. Vernon reached over and seized it. If it had a weapon inside, he wanted to make sure he got to it first.

Using his thigh as a shelf, he popped open the latch, all the while continuing to keep his gun trained on the Mini Cooper's driver. The case contained camera equipment and some packets of lens cleaners. There was also a burgundy-coloured passport sticking out of a side pocket; it had been issued by the United Kingdom. The photo inside matched the anxious face of the driver, and the name of the passport holder was identical to the name on the driver's licence and vehicle registration right down to the middle initial.

Looked like this Bear feller was who he claimed to be. But could he also be one of the bank bandits? Sheriff Purdue handed back the case. There was still the matter of the breathalyser test. He also threw in a Walk-and-Turn for good measure.

Thelonious T. Bear was as sober as a judge.

"So let's see some of them pictures then." A moment later Vernon found himself looking at images of his beloved home state on the camera's viewfinder. He had to admit, the critter took some mighty fine pictures. But he still had questions—and they could only be dealt with in a more official setting.

Although he didn't have the heart to up and arrest the little feller—especially seeing as his story seemed to add up, Vernon figured he'd better get the driver to follow him back the station and wait while he did some further checking. He might even call that publisher up in New York City whose name had been mentioned. It couldn't hurt to be thorough what with it coming up to a year for his next pay raise. Sheriff Purdue was already thinking about early retirement—he didn't want any black marks on his record. He wouldn't let this Thelonious T. Bear out of his sight until he knew everything there was to know and then some!

Chapter Eighteen

"Now LISTEN HERE, MAYNARD. Ah'm only callin' y'all as a courtesy, specially seein' as we go back a ways. Ah ain't lookin' for an argument, but this here feller's got one of them English flags on his vehicle, not a Confederate one! He's got a driver's licence from over in England too. Even his vehicle's registered thare!"

Thelonious overheard Sheriff Purdue's raised voice on the phone as he waited outside his office. The smell of coffee from a coffeemaker reached his nostrils, reminding him that he'd never had a chance to make use of those teabags he'd bought. He considered asking one of the office staff if he could have a cup, but decided against it. The less attention directed his way, the better.

There was a lengthy pause. When the sheriff finally resumed speaking, his tone was markedly less civil. "Ah talked to that publisher he says he works for and Ah'm tellin' y'all, this here Bear feller checks out!" There was another even lengthier silence, followed by an exasperated breath. "Ah don't know what y'all expect me to do here. Flag or no flag, Ah got no legal grounds to hold him. And Ah don't appreciate havin' folks tellin' me how to do my job neither!"

Sheriff Purdue chose that moment to close the door, leaving Thelonious sitting on a torturously hard chair, fretting over his fate. From what he'd managed to piece together from the sheriff's end of the conversation, he evidently resembled a bank robber wanted by the police. Eyewitnesses had also reported seeing a small car with a flag on the roof in the vicinity of one of the crimes committed by said bank robber, which undoubtedly explained why Thelonious was now cooling his heels at the sheriff's department. Apparently these people couldn't tell the difference between a Union Jack and a flag of the Confederate South.

The longer Thelonious sat there, the angrier he got. Bad enough getting a gun shoved in his muzzle, but he'd even had to submit to the indignity of a breathalyser test. When the results weren't to Sheriff Purdue's liking, Thelonious was then made to touch his nose with one claw and walk in a straight line—*and* do so on a public highway for the whole world to see. He'd nearly fallen over too, though not from drink as that gun-slinging sheriff was hoping, but because some hillbilly halfwit in a pickup truck had sounded his horn and shouted out something rude. If the sheriff hadn't been there, Thelonious would've given the driver a piece of his mind along with a piece of his furry fist!

Sheriff Purdue finally emerged from his office, though he didn't look too happy. Making a beeline for the coffeemaker, he poured a stream of muddy liquid into a mug with a sheriff's emblem on it and stood there drinking it until he suddenly seemed to remember Thelonious was still there. Topping up his mug, he stalked back to his office. "Y'all kin go," he barked over his shoulder, slamming the door so hard the building shook.

Scooting down from the chair, Thelonious trundled

toward the exit, all but daring anyone to stop him. He could feel Sheriff Purdue's eyes watching him from the office window as he levered himself up into the Mini's driver's seat. Let him look all he wanted. The fact that Thelonious had been stopped and detained because he bore some tenuous resemblance to a wanted criminal gave him street cred. Maybe he'd start wearing a baseball cap the wrong way round and trousers that hung halfway down his arse. Although the image of himself in gangsta mode provided some comic relief, it was short-lived. Thelonious had been treated abysmally. He needed to file an official complaint. He'd show these badge-wearing thugs they couldn't walk all over him!

Suddenly his mobile rang. "How's America's most wanted doing?" came Ira Goldfarb's Brooklyn bray.

Thelonious winced. He hated to think what must've been going through his publisher's mind when he'd got that phone call from Sheriff Purdue. Thelonious had only given his name to show that he was in the country on legitimate business—he'd never expected the sheriff to actually *phone* the man. Having that cannon shoved in his face by some wannabe Dirty Harry had scared Thelonious more than he cared to admit and his growly voice had tears in it as he told Ira Goldfarb what had happened. "Why, I could've been shot!" he added, swiping a pyjama sleeve across his damp nostrils. As Thelonious went on to vent his outrage and his determination to take Sheriff Purdue to task for his heavy-handed actions, he found himself cut off in mid-sentence.

"Take my advice and drop it," his publisher interrupted. "It's a seriously bad idea to mess with these redneck cops."

"But—"

"Thelonious, I know you're upset, but think about it a minute. You're not exactly in the best position here. For one thing, you're a bear. For another, you're a foreigner. America isn't as good at putting out the welcome mat as it used to be. You're in a part of the country that's teeming with right-wingers and rednecks—and most of these people didn't major in international relations, if ya know what I mean.

Though I suppose the one thing in your favour is, you're not
Muslim. At least I'm assuming you're not?"

Since Thelonious suspected his publisher was Jewish, he
quickly answered to the negative.

"Then trust me on this. Finish the book and move on to
something else. Don't let one bad experience overshadow all
the good. I mean, look how fabulous things turned out in
Norfolk?"

At this Thelonious broke into a coughing fit and had to
clamp his paw over the phone until it subsided. It was just as
well he'd never discussed his "fabulous" Norfolk experience
with Goldfarb or it might've marked the end of their
publishing relationship. Although he knew the man meant
well, Thelonious was embarrassed. He should've kept his
ursine gob shut instead of spouting off to Sheriff Purdue
about his big book deal, which—after out-of-pocket costs—
might leave him with enough to pay for a pulled pork
sandwich.

Thelonious decided to take his publisher's advice and let
it go. Nothing would come of it anyway. These shady
characters probably watched each other's backs and covered
up each other's wrongdoings all the time; filing a grievance
against a member of the good ol' boy cop network was asking
for trouble. Ira Goldfarb was right—Thelonious needed to
wrap things up and move on to the next project, provided
there would be one. He'd give it till the end of the week to
finish his book. After that he was out of here.

Instead of finding a motel as he'd originally intended,
Thelonious decided to spend the rest of the day driving
around the mountains photographing whatever took his
fancy. Now that he'd set himself a deadline, he needed to
make the most of every minute. Although he finally
changed out of his pyjamas in the Mini's back seat, he still
hadn't been able to wash. He'd been feeling itchy since he'd
left the campsite. He hoped he hadn't picked up any fleas.
Between those busybody squirrels and his nocturnal visitor
who'd left a steaming souvenir outside his tent, who knew

what might've set up shop in his fur?

When Thelonious saw the sign for a water mill, he headed in that direction, excited by the prospect of including an historical old mill in his book. Forty minutes later with still no mill in sight, he found himself pulling up to a minimart, reckoning someone there could give him directions since his SATNAV wasn't cooperating. A closer inspection indicated the minimart had closed for the day, as had the adjacent café. Even the fuel pumps had been shut down. There was an Amish furniture shop across from it, but it had gone out of business.

Thelonious continued on the same road; the mill was bound to show up sooner or later. The paved surface eventually changed to a couple of miles' worth of poorly maintained gravel that gave way to a dirt track, which disappeared into the woods. It looked like a fire road—and one that received very little use. Had he ended up in U.S. forestry land again?

It required some elaborate manoeuvring to turn around on the narrow track and Thelonious seriously underestimated how much room he had behind him. Before he could stop it from happening, he'd backed into a shallow gulley. The tyres spun in the soft soil, spewing plumes of red dust into the air. An SUV might've had the brawn to pull itself out of such a predicament, but the Mini Cooper wasn't having it. Thelonious clambered out of the tilting car, falling to his knees and receiving a muzzle-full of dusty Georgia clay. Brushing off his trousers, he checked his shirt pocket to make sure his phone hadn't fallen out. It was still there, but no matter which direction he turned, he couldn't get a signal. He tried to recall the last time he'd seen anything indicating human habitation, then realised he hadn't. Other than the disused fire road, it was wilderness.

It was a long walk back to the minimart; with his short legs, the light would be gone by the time he got there. Trying to flag down a passing vehicle in the dark didn't sound like a viable plan. Thelonious resolved to spend the night in the car and set off on foot in the morning. The minimart and café should be open by then—he could always use their phone to call a towing service, then wait for the tow so he could catch a ride back. The fact that he had a tent and sleeping bag that would've been a step up in comfort from the slanted interior of his Mini wasn't an option. After last night Thelonious wanted something more solid than nylon protecting him.

Suddenly he heard a machine-like ratcheting—and it was getting closer. A mud-caked pickup truck rattled toward him, its cargo bed overflowing with so much junk Thelonious expected to see a trail of debris behind it. He toddled into the road, waving his short arms in the air. "Stop!"

The brake pads grinded painfully as the truck came to a halt. The driver's-side door creaked open, and a lanky young man wearing bib overalls and a John Deere trucker cap hopped out.

"Evenin'!" he greeted. "What'all seems to be the trouble?" When Thelonious indicated the Mini, the driver grinned. "Y'all shore got yerself a problem," he concurred, spitting a glob of mucus into the dirt.

Still clutching his mobile, Thelonious said: "I can't get a signal. May I use your phone to call for a tow? If you have a signal, that is!"

"'Fraid Ah ain't got no phone, mister! Though that ain't no problem. Ah kin tow y'all out!"

Thelonious regarded the old wreck that had come to his aid. It didn't look fit to be on the road, let alone moonlight as a tow truck. He heard high-pitched giggles coming from the vehicle's cab as a couple of kiddies leaned out the passenger-side window to gawp at him. The boy looked like a spiteful little cur, his dark beady eyes filled with a meanness far beyond his years. The girl was the opposite, with perky blonde pigtails and a friendly open face.

"Daddy, Daddy!" she cried excitedly. "Kin we take the lil' baar home with us? He's awful cute!"

"Now Lilah-Mae, Ah gotta help this here feller with his car!" The father winked at Thelonious as if they shared a private joke. "We kin talk about it later," he added, as if to pacify her.

Talk about *what* later? wondered Thelonious, who was starting to get a bad feeling about his rescue team. Before he could think his way out of the situation, the pickup's driver was rummaging in the back of the cab, creating a terrific clatter as his head and torso vanished inside. He emerged holding a long steel chain with a large hook attached to each end. "Good thang Ah had this with me!" he said as he attached one end beneath the Mini's front bumper. Since he seemed to know what he was doing, Thelonious kept out of it. He just hoped his car wouldn't be damaged when it was over.

"Whatcha doin' way out here? Ain't nobody comes down this road but us folks who live here."

"*Live here?*"

The young man nodded as if he'd heard it a million times. "Yep. We's way back in them woods. See?" He pointed to the right of where the narrow track vanished into the woods. Thelonious followed his finger—and damned if he didn't see a second dirt track running parallel to the first. The angle of the sun had changed, which was why he hadn't noticed it earlier. He could see the warped metal frame of a swing set in amongst the trees—and behind it, part of a trailer. He wondered why there wasn't a mailbox by the road. Perhaps these people lived so far off the grid they never received mail. The alternative—that they didn't want anyone to know they were here—was too frightening to think about.

"We got us a doublewide," explained the young man, securing the other end of the chain to the rear of his pickup. "It ain't fancy, but it's home."

"Daddy, Daddy!" cried the little girl.

"Now punkin, y'all gotta let Daddy git on with his business, hear?"

"Y'all gonna pull that itty-bitty car out all by yerself, Pa?" chirped the boy. "Want me to help?"

"Nah, Ah think Ah kin manage. Y'all jus' look after your

sister for me till Ah's done."

Scowling, the boy stuck his tongue out at Thelonious, his expression pure evil.

Hopping back into his truck, the father shouted at Thelonious to start the engine and shift into neutral. Because of the angle in which the Mini was stuck, Thelonious had to crawl his way into the driver's seat, its built-up cushion creating an additional hurdle. By the time he'd got himself belted in, he was panting. He signalled with a wave of his paw that he was ready.

With a metallic wheeze, the pickup inched forward until the chain grew taut, whereupon Thelonious felt a sudden jerk. A moment later both car and driver were bumping up the incline, with Thelonious clinging to the steering wheel as he tried to keep the front tyres from being knocked out of alignment. At last the Mini was free of the gulley.

The children cheered. "Way to go, Pa!" cried the boy, who continued to eye Thelonious as if he wanted to kill and dismember him—and not necessarily in that order.

Hopping down from the truck, the man unhooked the chain from both vehicles. "Y'all good to go, mister!" He touched the faded brim of his cap in a mock salute.

Thelonious jumped out of the driver's seat, too embarrassed to be seen using his pulley device, wincing in pain as he landed too hard on his left foot. "I don't know how to thank you!" he said, reaching into his trouser pocket for his wallet. The least he could do was to offer the man some money; the family looked as though they could use it.

"Now y'all put that right back where it come from." The pickup's driver waved away the twenty-dollar bill in Thelonious's outthrust paw. "Ah's happy to help!"

"I appreciate it," croaked Thelonious, genuinely touched by the young man's kindness. It was heartening to know that not every good turn came with a price tag attached.

"Daddy, kin we, kin we?" the little girl's piping voice interrupted.

"Kin we *what*, punkin?"

"Kin we take the lil' baar home with us? Ah wanna play with him!"

"Betcha he squeaks if'n he gits squeezed!" chimed the boy, a nasty gleam in his eye.

The children's father began to laugh so hard Thelonious thought he could hear his bones rattling. Suddenly the young man was eyeballing him with an expression that hadn't been there earlier. Thelonious took a few steps back, his newfound sense of all being right with the world spiralling away from him. He didn't like the way the man was holding that chain— as if he wanted to latch it around Thelonious's neck and parade him about like a circus animal.

"Daddy!" The little girl's voice turned to a tearful wail. "Ah wanna play with the baar!"

"Me too, pa!" added the boy.

Thelonious hadn't travelled all the way to America to become the resident plaything for a pair of psychopathic hillbilly tots. He weighed his chances of getting back inside the Mini before the family descended on him; they weren't good. When he heard the screech of rusty door hinges he suddenly thought of all the things he still wanted to do in his life but hadn't had a chance to. The little boy had pushed open the door of the truck, intent on getting out. A dull thud followed as his sister landed in the dirt, having either fallen out or been pushed. Thelonious suspected the latter. She began to shriek.

The young man went running over to scoop her up in his arms. "Y'all gonna git a whuppin' soon's we git home!" he shouted at his son. The girl turned up the volume, her satisfied smirk going unseen by her devoted father. The boy stared darkly at Thelonious as if he were to blame.

"Jeb!" A shrill female voice yelled from the woods. "Y'all git them young'uns in here right now! It's bath night!"

Taking advantage of the distraction, Thelonious clawed his way up onto the driver's seat, grateful he'd left the engine running. Within seconds the Mini Cooper was shimmying down the dirt road on its now-misaligned front tyres, a budding serial killer in need of a bath running after it.

Chapter Nineteen

**"Animal Dwarf Bandits" Rob Dogwood Falls Bank!
Bystander Shot!**
—Front page headline from the *Appalachian Reporter*

SHERIFF VERNON PURDUE ISSUED a "Be On The Lookout"
alert for Thelonious T. Bear, citizen of the United Kingdom.

> Age: unknown
> Height: short
> Weight: tubby
> Physical description: furry
> ~~Race:~~ Species: bear

Reports had been coming in that an individual fitting Bear's
description had been seen in Dogwood Falls at the
supermarket and at Big Al's Sporting Goods the day before

the robbery and shooting at Great Mountain Bank, where Bear had also been seen withdrawing money. The hidden camera inside the ATM machine had filmed him making the transaction, after which he'd bared his teeth at the lens and growled in a threatening manner.

Maybe it was circumstantial evidence and maybe it wasn't, but the sheriff figured he'd better cover his behind seeing as he had the critter sitting right outside his office, only to let him go. Not that he believed for a minute this Thelonious T. Bear could be a bank robber. He'd practically shit in his pants when Vernon told him he'd been driving with a snake on top of his car! The little feller was probably long gone by now, which was okay with the sheriff. Let someone else worry about bank robbers and pyjama-wearing bears driving foreign cars. He'd done what he needed to do and could now get on with the other business of the day.

Being a Wednesday, Sadie's Home Cookin' over on the main highway had their shrimp and grits lunch special. Sheriff Purdue hadn't missed a single Wednesday since he'd joined the Oakfield County Sheriff's Department. Miss Sadie always served him an extra helping too, what with him being sheriff. It went a ways toward convincing him to be merciful when her husband got caught drunk driving. Not that Vernon was one of those on-the-take sheriffs like some others whose names he wouldn't mention. He was just being a good Christian helping a fellow Christian. He saw it as his duty, especially since Miss Sadie and Dwayne went to the same church as the Purdue family. Whenever he took his pickup to be serviced at Dwayne's garage, he always made sure to give Dwayne a stern talking to about the evils of liquor, though he never went so far as to suggest he go to an A.A. meeting. It was up to the Lord to make Dwayne see the error of his ways, not Vernon Purdue. Since nobody'd been injured or killed, it proved that Jesus was watching over Dwayne. Though the sheriff suspected Miss Sadie did a lot of praying.

Vernon hadn't even got a foot out the door before the phone on his desk rang. He knew he should've ignored it, but curiosity always got the better of him. The call wouldn't have been put through unless it was important, seeing as it was his lunch break. Instead of being treated to Miss Sadie's delicious shrimp and grits, Sheriff Purdue was treated to the marble-munching drawl of Sheriff Maynard Grizzle, who sounded like a rabid coon chasing an injured rabbit.

Lord have mercy. If only he'd left a few minutes earlier!

"Afternoon, Maynard. What kin Ah do for y'all?" Vernon didn't bother to hide his annoyance. "Ah'm just on my way out." He hoped his caller would get the message, but Grizzle was on the warpath. Apparently he'd seen Vernon's BOLO and had plenty to say about it.

"Ah'm tellin' y'all, this here's our man!" Sheriff Grizzle shouted into the phone. "But 'stead of lockin' him up, y'all jus' let him waltz on outta thare!"

Sheriff Purdue experienced a powerful dislike for his counterpart a few counties south. Maynard Grizzle was the kind of cop that gave Southern cops a bad name, especially those in the great state of Georgia. Crooked, pig-headed and stupid—that summed up Grizzle and his breed. Vernon hoped he'd never become another Sheriff Grizzle, despite the occasional "convenient" traffic ticket he encouraged his deputies to issue to motorists. But his county needed revenue, and his deputies needed to keep busy.

"Now y'all just listen here a minute!" Vernon was fit to be tied. "At the time Ah had no legal reason to hold the feller. Ah questioned him and Ah even checked his job reference. Hell, Ah did everythin' short of checkin' his underpants for skid marks! As for his vehicle, it didn't have no Confederate flag on it. It had one of what they call Union Jacks from England. That's over in Europe, in case y'all didn't know!"

Why, oh why had he issued that BOLO? Now he looked like some idiot cop who'd allowed a dangerous criminal to escape. He'd never live it down if this Bear feller was one of the "animal dwarf bandits." Early retirement was looking better by the minute. Maybe he'd move to one of those golf communities in Florida. Not that Vernon played golf....

But Sheriff Grizzle refused to back down. Instead he continued to argue that the individual wanted for questioning in the Dogwood Falls bank heist was the same individual wanted for questioning in the Stumpville bank heist—*and* that this individual drove a car with a Confederate flag on the roof until even Vernon doubted what he'd seen with his own eyes. Though one thing he *did* know—the feller he'd questioned was definitely foreign; he'd had a hard time understanding him with that accent. Vernon had also checked his identity and verified his employment, which was more than that lazy no-account Maynard Grizzle had done.

"Ah don't give a rat's bee-hind if he's some dadburned foreigner!" countered Sheriff Grizzle. "That makes it even worse!" Vernon heard phlegm being hacked up, followed by the sound of spitting. "Ah knows guilt when Ah sees it!" resumed Grizzle. "And that critter's guilty as sin!"

"Do what y'all gotta do, Maynard. Ah really need to git back to business here."

But Sheriff Grizzle continued as if Vernon had never spoken. "Ah'm settin' up a conference call with every sheriff in the state," he said, his voice rising with excitement. "We's gonna nail this here—what'd y'all say his name is a'gin?"

"Thelonious T. Bear."

"Right, Thee-lone-yus Bear. As Ah was sayin', we's gonna nail this here Thee-lone-yus Bear and all them other thievin' murderin' midgets in his gang! They ain't gonna keep runnin' roughshod over us, no sirree, Bob!"

A conference call? If Vernon didn't know better, he'd think the sheriff had bigger fish to fry than those in his dead-end county. Though there were plenty of Sheriff Grizzles already—Georgia was crawling with pea-brained rednecks in positions of authority all the way up to the state legislature. Let him have his big conference call—Vernon wanted no part of it. The less he had to do with this Bear business, the better. Hopefully by next week it would all be forgotten.

But there was no listening to reason when it came to Maynard Grizzle. The man didn't have the good sense God gave a goat. Holding the receiver away from his ear, Vernon issued an occasional mumble of acknowledgment to Grizzle's rant, silently praying that Miss Sadie wouldn't run out of shrimp and grits by the time he got there. Without realising it, one of his mumbles had just committed him to the date and time of Sheriff Grizzle's conference call.

Chapter Twenty

SHERIFF MAYNARD GRIZZLE'S CONFERENCE call didn't turn out to be as major an event as he'd anticipated, though it *did* attract a handful of sheriffs—mostly those from counties so lacking in criminal activity that any excuse for excitement was welcome. Therefore when *Pinewood Times-Courier* reporter Nate Jessop got wind of it and begged permission to sit in on the call, the request was met with an immediate *yes*.

Nate listened via speaker phone in Grizzle's office as the sheriff held court, leaning back in his swivel chair with his boot-clad feet resting on the corner of his desk. The front of his uniform was speckled with crumbs and he chased them around with a saliva-dampened fingertip, returning them to his mouth. A basket of apple fritters sat on top of a photocopier that hadn't functioned since the 1990s. Nate wouldn't be offered one and he was too intimidated to ask.

These days Sheriff Grizzle was more than happy to give

his time to the press. He even took phone calls at home. The more his name showed up in print or got mentioned on TV and radio, the more attention the bigger news media outlets gave him, positioning him as a man of importance—a man who was *going places*. Sheriff Purdue's suspicions hadn't been too far off the mark. Maynard Grizzle *did* have his sights set on something grander than being the sheriff of a small rural county. But no one could've predicted what that would ultimately be, not even Sheriff Grizzle himself.

Suddenly everyone seemed to be coming out of the woodwork with sightings of a sinister gun-toting dwarf-bear who drove a small car with a Confederate flag on the roof. There were even sightings in the neighbouring states of Alabama, Tennessee and the Carolinas, though these claims were eventually dismissed as bogus. Details once pedestrian took on kaleidoscopic colours, painting the diminutive subject in shades of evil that would've made John Dillinger envious. Despite the fact that no one had actually *seen* the now-identified Thelonious T. Bear carrying a gun (let alone a sharp pencil), that didn't stop concerned citizens from including it in their reports. It was common knowledge that the "animal dwarf bandits" had been armed with old-fashioned Tommy Guns during their bank heists, so it stood to reason Thelonious had one too. Even Nate Jessop became convinced that the little car he'd been following had a gun mounted in the rear window, though he couldn't be certain if it had a Type C drum magazine like those described by eyewitnesses to the robberies.

The most recent character to add his voice to the din was an old-timer who owned a country store in the North Georgia Mountains. Although he didn't have a record of the transaction to verify the exact date and time of the encounter (he'd forgotten to ring up the sale for the tax man), he recalled a customer matching Thelonious T. Bear's description behaving in a threatening manner toward him, which included forcing him to pose for photographs.

"Them Native Indian folks think you're stealin' their soul

if'n y'all take a picture of 'em!" the proprietor told a TV news reporter from Atlanta, his filmy eyes going wide with fright. "What's the world comin' to when we got dangerous criminals runnin' all over the place? Ah shoulda shot that dadburned critter when Ah had a chance!" he cried, showing off his missing front teeth. He reached beneath the counter for an old pump-action shotgun, waving it proudly in front of the camera.

The interview was aired on the station's evening and night-time news broadcasts and again on the early morning and noon editions the next day. The interview also appeared in print in a slightly different version in the mountain town's community newspaper, misquoting the old-timer as saying he'd been forced at gunpoint to pose for pornographic photos.

Thelonious T. Bear had now become Public Enemy Number One.

Chapter Twenty-one

"ON THE GROUND! *NOW!*"

Thelonious had just finished loading his gear into his Mini Cooper when two sheriff's deputies descended on him with guns drawn. The next thing he knew his muzzle was being mashed into the pavement as the stockier of the pair sat on top of him, ramming a knee into his back. He couldn't breathe. It felt as if a grand piano had landed on him. Thelonious heard the crackling of a two-way radio. Suddenly he noticed several patrol cars parked at haphazard angles in the motel's car park.

They hadn't been there a minute ago.

At some point during the melee Thelonious's deerstalker hat tumbled off. When he tried to reach for it, he yelped as something hard was jabbed into his side. "One more move and y'all gittin' Tasered!" threatened the deputy on his back. Before he could explain that he'd merely been trying to retrieve his hat, the deputy was patting him from the top of his now-bare head to the bottom of his trainers, even skimming his groin. Thelonious had never felt so violated in his life! But there was nothing he could do. He was powerless against this ham-fisted bully with a badge.

Whipping Thelonious's short arms behind him, the deputy fastened his furry wrists together with a plastic cable tie, cinching it so tight his paws went numb. "Okay, let's go!"

The bones in Thelonious's neck made an ominous popping sound as he found himself being yanked up from the ground to a standing position. He hoped his neck hadn't been injured or any of his ribs cracked. "My hat!" he cried. It was right by his foot. But the other deputy had his gun drawn—and Thelonious's torso was its target.

Thelonious had his rights bellowed at him before being hauled to a patrol car and hurled into the back seat, the door barely missing his foot as it slammed shut. The back of the vehicle felt like a cage and stank of human sweat and onions. As he stared out the grimy window to see if anyone had retrieved his hat, Thelonious noticed the clerk from reception watching timidly from the lobby. After a while he came outside to speak to one of the deputies, who pumped his hand as if he were a returning war hero. They were then joined by a familiar-looking figure who strode over to add his own enthusiastic handshake to the celebration, even clapping the motel's employee on the back. As he was about to return to the lobby, the clerk glared at Thelonious with such loathing one might've thought he'd been arrested for the murder of the young man's grandmother. Suddenly Thelonious realised where he'd seen the new arrival before.

A moment later Sheriff Vernon Purdue was squeezing himself behind the steering wheel of the patrol car, the metal grill behind his head keeping him safe from dangerous criminals occupying the back seat. He mumbled something into his radio, to which a garbled female voice responded.

Thelonious T. Bear was about to receive a personal escort to jail courtesy of the Oakfield County Sheriff.

Chapter Twenty-two

"Animal Dwarf Bandits" Bank Robbery Suspect Arrested!
—Front page headline from the *Pinewood Times-Courier, Special Edition*
By Nathan Jessop, Senior News Reporter

The recent string of armed bank robberies committed by a violent gang of little people wearing animal masks may finally be reaching an end. Thanks to a state-wide manhunt spearheaded by Pinewood County Sheriff Maynard Grizzle, a suspect was arrested yesterday in the mountain town of Beaumont Gap in Oakfield County.

Pinewood County and Oakfield County Sheriff's Departments have identified the suspect as Thelonious T. Bear, a citizen of the United Kingdom. Bear was seen in the area where at least two of the robberies took place. He was later identified by Polly DuKane, a waitress at A Taste of Heaven in downtown Stumpville, where Bear ate fried chicken right before the hold-up took place at *Stumpville Bank and Trust*. His car, which has a Confederate flag painted on the roof, was also seen in the vicinity of the crimes. Bear claims to be a photographer on assignment in Georgia. He closely matches the description of one of the bandits. The other three remain at large.

Sheriff Grizzle is working closely with law enforcement in Oakfield County to have Bear returned to Pinewood County. "I want to urge everybody to remain calm and let us do our job," the sheriff told Stumpville residents at a town-hall meeting with Mayor Jarvis Calhoun. "As long as I'm in charge, folks got nothing to worry about!"

More arrests are expected to follow.

"I DEMAND TO SPEAK TO MY LAWYER!"

Thelonious repeated the refrain to everyone he came into contact with, unaware that he'd also included the Oakfield County Sheriff's Department janitor, who'd recently arrived from Guatemala. The mop and bucket should've been a giveaway, but Thelonious had been too distraught to notice. That fact that he didn't have a lawyer added to his worries. He was in a foreign country—he didn't want to make things worse by saying or doing the wrong thing. His demands went ignored. Instead he found himself being shuffled from room to room, first to get his mugshot taken, then bundled off to be fingerprinted—or rather, *paw*-printed. The tissue he'd been given to wipe off the ink did nothing but smear it into his fur. His paws now looked two-toned, the lustrous brown tipped with black. He needed soap and water, not a glorified piece of loo roll!

Rather than being taken to see someone in charge, Thelonious was abandoned inside a small cell. Enclosed on three sides by steel bars, the lockup had a cinder-block wall at the rear with a nasty brown splatter on it. This glorified cage came equipped with a stainless-steel toilet and sink, a bench, and an old drunk who reeked of whiskey and piss. The drunk was the only thing that hadn't been bolted down. As for the lidless toilet, it sat out in the open like a piece of furniture in a stage play. Thelonious knew he could never use it, not even if he were desperate. Maybe this explained why his cellmate smelled as he did, preferring the privacy of his trousers to a public display of his bodily functions.

As the drunk snored away on the concrete floor without a care in the world, Thelonious toddled back and forth in the confined space, raging inwardly at this latest injustice to come his way. He felt like punching something, Sheriff Purdue's nose being top of the list. Weren't there laws about how long someone could be held without being charged with an offence? Surely a deputy would come by sooner or later to let him out, even if only to call that lawyer he didn't have. Climbing onto the bench, Thelonious sat slumped forward with his head in his paws, which had finally begun to get some circulation back now that they were no longer cinched together. He felt terribly naked without his hat. He wondered if he'd ever see it again.

They hadn't even allowed him to lock the Mini or engage the alarm. His camera equipment and laptop were there for anyone to steal, not to mention the car itself. Any halfway competent thief could probably hotwire it. As for Thelonious's phone, that had been confiscated along with his wallet and the laces from his trainers. Did they seriously think he was going to try to hang himself?

Suddenly he heard footsteps. One of the deputies Thelonious had seen from when he'd first been brought in approached. Finally someone in authority had figured out he'd been arrested by mistake—heads were probably rolling already! As the cell door opened, he scooted down from the bench in preparation to leave. But instead of escorting Thelonious out of the cell, the deputy strolled over to the drunk and kicked him in the side.

"Wha-wha—" stammered the old man as he tried to roll out of harm's way.

"Y'all's missus is here to take your drunk ass home. Now git!" snarled the deputy.

"My missus?"

"That's what Ah said!"

"What about me?" cried Thelonious. "And what about my hat?"

The deputy glared in Thelonious's direction, clearly annoyed at having his fun interrupted. "We's waitin' on Sheriff Grizzle."

"*Sheriff Grizzle?*" Was this still about the mix-up with his car? Thelonious couldn't believe that a Union Jack could be the cause of so much trouble.

"That's what Ah said. Now set yerself down and shut up! Ah ain't tellin' y'all ag'in, hear?"

As if for good measure, the deputy launched another kick at the old man. "Git your drunk bee-hind off the floor before Ah stick my gun up it! Ah'm sick of y'all comin' in here every dang week stinkin' up the place."

The drunk managed to heave himself up into an unsteady likeness of a standing position. He staggered out of the cell with the deputy, who kept prodding him in the back to get a move on. Thelonious worried he'd be forgotten now that his cell-mate was gone. At least the smelly old drunk had a wife to come to his rescue; he had no one. Suddenly his nostrils began to quiver. He smelled meat—and unless his reliable olfactory system deceived him, it was pork. *Barbecued* pork. Thelonious's belly rumbled with hunger. The only thing he'd eaten today was a granola bar from his camping stash. The smell became stronger. A moment later the deft-footed deputy returned.

"Thare's been a delay," he mumbled through gory mouthfuls of pork. Barbecue sauce smeared his lips like blood.

"A delay?" croaked Thelonious.

"Yep. Sheriff Grizzle's runnin' late. And we ain't rightly sure what time he'll git here neither."

"Does this mean I can go?" It hadn't occurred to Thelonious that Grizzle was actually on his way here. From what the deputy had said earlier, he'd assumed it was paperwork holding things up.

"Not till Sheriff Grizzle gits here. He's takin' y'all back to

Pinewood County with him."

Thelonious didn't like the sound of that. But before he could find out more, the deputy sauntered off with his barbecued pork sandwich, leaving the prisoner in his cage.

Chapter Twenty-three

As THELONIOUS SAT IN A JAIL cell a couple hundred miles to the north, the town of Stumpville was hit for the second time by the armed gang of little people wearing animal masks. This time their departure didn't go quite so smoothly.

A Taste of Heaven's Miss Polly happened to be standing outside the diner smoking a cigarette when a small car carrying four diminutive passengers drove slowly past. It double-parked in front of Stumpville Bank and Trust, at which point the vehicle's doors flew open. Recognising the bear-faced fellow climbing down from the passenger seat, she ran inside to phone the sheriff's department, nearly wetting herself with excitement as she reported what she'd seen, adding that this particular individual had stuck his gun out the car window and aimed it at her—a fiction she continued to maintain until she'd come to believe it herself.

Sheriff Grizzle had been about to leave for the North

Georgia Mountains to pick up a suspect in the bank robberies when the call came in. He sprang into action, descending on the scene as if he were leading a SWAT team instead of his motley crew of overweight and out-of-shape deputies.

Which was how a shootout between the bank bandits and Pinewood County Sheriff's deputies ensued.

Passers-by took cover behind parked cars or hid inside businesses. Many had started praying, making vows they could never keep. Those who'd sought safety at A Taste of Heaven joined Miss Polly at the window, peering cautiously out as patrol cars received a hailstorm of bullets from the robbers' Tommy Guns, the sound of bullets piercing steel and shattering glass drowning out the diner's piped-in country music. As the pavement glittered with broken glass from the vehicles shot-out windows, a police radio crackled with its last utterance before shorting out completely.

That radio belonged to Sheriff Grizzle's patrol car. It had been parked closest to the bank's entrance, thereby attracting the wrath of the robber in the goat mask. The sheriff had left the engine running; oily black smoke haemorrhaged out from beneath the ruined front end until the owner of the feed store finally came running over with a fire extinguisher, though only after the robbers had fled in their getaway car. The fire department had been alerted, but being a volunteer service the men couldn't be rounded up in time. Although no one was seriously injured, the shootout did result in a broken arm for one of the deputies, who'd tripped over the foot of another, falling and landing on his arm and breaking it in two places.

None of the bank robbers was apprehended.

Miss Polly was hailed as a hero for being the one to sound the alert. But the real honour went to Sheriff Maynard Grizzle, whose swift actions in dispatching his team to the scene had, in his words, "showed them no-good midgets who's boss around here!" The fact that his actions might've been considered extreme—particularly with regard to putting lives at risk—was never mentioned. In a special ceremony on the steps of Stumpville City Hall, Mayor Jarvis Calhoun presented Sheriff Grizzle with the key to the city. It was the first time anyone had been awarded one. The whole town turned out, including "eligible bachelor" Jed Pickett, the one-legged Vietnam War veteran.

And *Pinewood Times-Courier*'s newly promoted senior news reporter Nathan Jessop was there to report on every glittering moment of it.

Chapter Twenty-four

A log cabin in the woods

"RAISE!"

A bundle of twenty-dollar bills held together with a currency strap joined several others heaped in the centre of a pine table that looked as if it had been scored with a knife and used as an ashtray. The sound of liquid being poured resonated in the smoky room as the gambler who'd upped the stakes splashed three fingers of Kentucky bourbon into a chipped glass, drinking it down in one go. He smacked his lips in satisfaction, his eyes trained on the pile of money.

"Fold!" called a voice roughened from years of tobacco smoke and hard drinking. Cards slammed down onto the table.

"Since you got nothing else to do, get us another bottle from the kitchen," ordered the player who'd raised the bet. He took a puff from an illegally obtained Cuban cigar. "Or better yet, we got any of that hooch left?"

"You mean the stuff from that crazy old farmer? Nah. We finished the last of it."

"Shit. That white lightning practically set my balls on fire, it was so good." As if stirred by the memory, the player reached down and scratched his testicles. The other players stared at him in disgust.

Chair legs scraped the worn pine floor as the player who'd folded clambered down from his seat and went into the kitchen. The sound of a cabinet door being opened, then slammed shut reached the other players at the card table. The defeated gambler returned with a bottle of 140-proof Kentucky bourbon, which he'd already opened and taken a swig from. He climbed back up onto his chair to wait out the game. He still had plenty of money left for the next one, and the next one after that. They *all* had plenty of money. Betting relieved the boredom until they went out and got more money. Whoever said crime didn't pay sure had shit for brains.

A haze of smoke hung over the poker players like grey smog. The quartet shared similar height and build, ranging in age from early-forties to late fifties. Extra thick cushions padded the seats of their chairs, elevating them so they could reach the action without difficulty. The gamblers all had their own supply of cash either in neat stacks at their elbows or stored in duffle bags on the floor by their feet. The better who'd raised the stakes kept his loot inside a Miss Kitty backpack—and no one dared to say a word about it. "Card!" he demanded.

The dealer scrutinised him from behind a rubber chicken mask. "Sure you're good for it?"

"'Course I'm good for it, asshole!"

"Just checking," said the dealer, expertly skimming a card from the top of the deck. He sent it flying across the table, where it was promptly examined.

"Raise!" the player shouted again. He took another puff from his cigar, exhaling the smoke toward the dealer.

"Fold!" came an answering shout as another player bailed from the game. It was now between the gambler with the cigar and the dealer in the chicken mask.

The player who'd bailed from the game hopped down from his chair, his round face screwed up in disgust. "I need some air," he muttered, slamming out the front door. He stood on the rickety front porch, watching the rooster weathervane twirling in the breeze. He hated the stupid thing, but one of the guys had a thing for poultry. The cabin had paintings of roosters and chickens all over the place, even in the john.

A garden hose lay uncoiled on the ground. Because of last night's thunderstorm, it was now half-drowned in mud. Any more rain and they wouldn't be able to find it. He supposed he should wind it back into its thingumabob, though he didn't see why it was always down to *him* to do these things. He also supposed he should do something about replacing the mailbox since no one else seemed to be making any effort to do so, but since the mail carrier was putting everything in the newspaper holder he didn't see the point.

The bugs kept buzzing him so he went back inside the smoky cabin. Four Tommy Guns leaned against a pot-bellied stove that provided an extra source of heat for the cabin in winter. As he headed toward them, the posture of the two remaining poker players stiffened, then relaxed after they saw him remove a cloth from the pocket of his trousers. Grabbing up one of the guns, he took it with him to the sofa and made himself comfortable. Propping one undersized foot against the edge of a scarred coffee table, he started to polish the vintage weapon, humming an old Johnny Cash song about a man in prison. It always relaxed him when he had a gun in his hands.

A copy of the *Pinewood Times-Courier* had been left on the coffee table along with a souvenir ashtray from Miami Beach. It overflowed with ash and crushed cigar ends. Some of the ash had spilled onto the newspaper, partially obscuring the police mugshot emblazoned across the front. A pair of shell-shocked eyes stared out from a furry visage.

Suspect Released in "Animal Dwarf Bandits" Bank Robberies. Culprits Still at Large!

Epilogue

New Stars are Born in...*Stumpville?*
—Front page headline from *Variety*

Stumpville, Georgia
"Y'ALL EAT UP ALL THEM GRITS, HEAR?" Miss Polly told the pimply faced teen as she placed a steaming bowl of grits on the table. It accompanied a plate of fried chicken, sweet "tater" fries, fried okra, homemade biscuits and a large glass of sweet tea—otherwise known as the "Bank Robbers Special" at A Taste of Heaven in downtown Stumpville. Turning to face the camera, she grinned, showing off her newly whitened teeth. "That's why our Southern boys are so handsome and manly—it's them grits!"

"Okay, cut!" shouted the director of America's newest reality TV series. "Good work, people!"

Scowling, the teenaged boy pushed away the bowl. He

hated grits. He also hated fried chicken, having seen the way chickens were treated at the local poultry farms. If he had his way, he'd go vegan, but his folks refused to pay extra for vegan-certified food products. So he stuck to vegetables, which made everyone at school think he was gay.

Road to Stumpville soared through the ratings roof the week of its debut. Although dismissed by critics as "a flash in the pan," the series managed to hold on to its high ratings and keep its viewers, with more tuning in each week. Not only was it renewed by the network before the third episode, sponsors were parting with huge sums of money to pay for a time slot in which to advertise their wares. *Road to Stumpville* was the first prime-time one-hour television series to be shot, edited and put on the airwaves within a turnaround time that everyone in the business claimed was impossible, which might've explained why it wasn't as polished as the competition. But *Road to Stumpville* had a winning formula: a cast of fools who had no idea they were fools. Not only was America laughing with them, America was laughing *at* them.

The series turned out to be a bigger hit than the Hollywood TV execs had dreamed possible, even grabbing ratings higher than the combined figures for the category of programming these same execs privately called "Hillbilly Entertainment Shows." America's cultural psyche had been undergoing major changes the last few years—and *Road to Stumpville* was a perfect fit. Of course these very same TV executives thrilled by the show's success wouldn't dare say what they *really* thought of it unless they were behind closed doors with like-minded colleagues. Even the series' producer had no idea.

A Taste of Heaven's Miss Polly catapulted to fame as America's surrogate aunt. Even rich kids from Beverly Hills could be seen sporting T-shirts with her name and face plastered across the front. "Bless your heart!" became America's official slogan, climbing its way out of the Deep South and reaching all the way to Alaska and Hawaii. Inner-city communities in Chicago, Oakland and Los Angeles were also feeling the love, with a hip-hop group from Compton recording "The Miss Polly Rap," which went straight to number one on the Billboard charts in multiple categories, including Country. Miss Polly's endorsement showed up on everything from budget-priced face bronzer to budget-priced frying pans. Thanks to quick-thinking New York publisher Ira Goldfarb, she even landed a book deal to do a cookbook featuring recipes for grits. America couldn't get enough of her.

Mayor Jarvis Calhoun, whom TV execs initially dismissed as only being worthy of the occasional cameo, also became a major player—the small-town mayor to whom everyone went in time of need or crisis. Whether it was refereeing a dispute between neighbours over a fallen tree or counselling someone's son on the evils of premarital sex, the mayor was the air that filled Stumpville's lungs. His inflated sense of his own importance seemed to add to his appeal rather than putting viewers off as Hollywood feared. The fact that he was married *and* engaging in sexual congress with Miss Polly DuKane never made its way into the storyline. *Road to Stumpville* was billed as "wholesome Christian entertainment for the entire family"—and marital infidelity didn't qualify as wholesome viewing material in the mind of series' producer Hank Ayers, a Christian man from small-town Missouri.

A graduate in media studies, thirty-one-year-old Ayers was determined to return family values to American television. He'd grown up watching old reruns of *Father Knows Best*, *The Andy Griffith Show* and *Leave It to Beaver*—TV shows where the husband was head of the household, the wife looked after home and hearth, and children were taught to always obey their elders. Although he longed for the America of the past, he could still influence what Americans watched on their televisions, laptops, tablets and smartphones *today*. "The medium is the message," communication theorist Marshall McLuhan once said—and Hank planned to use his chosen medium to get that message across. The Lord in His infinite wisdom had chosen *him* to right some of the wrongs

Mitzi Szereto & Teddy Tedaloo

in this great country—and Hank Ayers was up to the task. *Road to Stumpville* was only the beginning!

Of course no television series filmed in Stumpville, Georgia would be complete without its own Sheriff Andy Taylor or—in this case—Sheriff Maynard Grizzle, who took to the spotlight like a randy rooster to the hen house. One might've assumed a pea-sized hamlet like Stumpville wouldn't need a sheriff to be patrolling its streets very often, especially when other parts of the county were plagued with a methamphetamine problem—a problem no one ever discussed, but which nevertheless grew worse each year. Aside from the two bank robberies committed by the still at-large "animal dwarf bandits," nothing criminally noteworthy had happened in Stumpville since Mayor Calhoun's thirteen-year-old niece had stolen a Snickers bar from the Dollar General. Yet whether on duty or off, Sheriff Grizzle could be found in Stumpville's postage-stamp downtown *and* in front of the cameras until Hank Ayers was finally obliged to have him written into the script as a main character.

Although *Road to Stumpville* was billed as a "reality" series, like most in the genre there was very little reality actually in it. Much of what took place was staged, albeit with amateurs who not only played themselves, but earned considerably less than professional actors—or at least they did until the cast members became America's darlings. As for the TV execs back in Hollywood, they'd never seen such a bunch of backwoods hams in their lives. But Hank Ayers and the rest of America loved it.

After his promotion to senior news reporter at the *Pinewood Times-Courier* (while still remaining the *only* reporter), the newly rebranded Nathan Jessop and his boss's niece finally made plans to tie the knot, which was just as well considering he'd got her pregnant. Being a minnow in an ocean of big fish, Nathan knew when he was defeated. The gang of robbers had never been caught. After their last bank heist in the Smokey Mountains of Tennessee, they'd gone underground, leaving Nathan with nothing to report on

181

except farm news, church news and random bits of crime such as chicken thieving and illegally dumped furniture. He blamed himself for not being good enough—something his intended Miss Mandy did nothing to discourage, since it meant he'd finally given up on leaving the area to join the journalism big leagues.

Nathan decided to be practical about it. So maybe he *wasn't* going to be some high-flying reporter at a big-city newspaper, but by staying local and marrying the boss's niece, he had a real chance of taking over the *Pinewood Times-Courier* when old man Clemson retired. And Miss Mandy wasn't all that bad, considering. Even her kid was tolerable…in small doses. Anyways, little Clem would be starting school soon. Clem Clemson—that was the kid's name. It was no skin off Nathan's nose if Clem Clemson didn't become Clem *Jessop* after the wedding. As far as he was concerned, his soon-to-be wife's son by another man could keep his mother's family name. Old man Clemson had been worried Nathan would make a big stink about it and when he didn't, it had won him a few bonus points with his boss and future uncle-in-law. However, the *real* reason for Nathan's relaxed attitude had nothing to do with sentiment. He kept hoping that one day the kid's father would show up and start paying child support, especially once he found out that little Clem hadn't been legally adopted by Miss Mandy's new husband.

But Nathan Jessop would ultimately be blessed with many more mouths to feed thanks to Miss Mandy's fertile womb until he no longer even remembered Clem Clemson wasn't his child by blood.

As for Mr. Clemson, he remained publisher and editor-in-chief of the *Pinewood Times-Courier* and showed no sign of retiring.

"Take my advice and git outta town. Better yet, git outta Georgia!"

Sheriff Purdue's words were still fresh in Thelonious's mind as he drove toward the Tennessee border. Tennessee was the nearest place that *wasn't* Georgia—and right now that was good enough for Thelonious.

No one at the Oakfield County Sheriff's Department had offered an explanation. One minute he was locked inside a cell, the next he was being shooed toward the exit like a flea-riddled cat that had sneaked inside. Thelonious had collected his Mini Cooper from the impound yard, relieved to find nothing missing or damaged. He'd even got his hat back, though it looked as if it had been run over by a lorry. From there he'd stopped at a fast-food restaurant for something to eat and to use the free Wi-Fi to search for anything that might explain what had just happened to him. Thelonious found plenty to fill in the blanks, including several articles in some cheesy little newspaper from the county where he'd been stalked by the driver of a red pickup truck, harassed by a redneck sheriff, and terrorised by a religious zealot with a rattlesnake. After that he didn't need Sheriff Purdue's advice to send him packing!

"Animal dwarf bandits" the press called them. Whatever they were, Thelonious couldn't help but feel a vicarious sense of retribution. He was willing to bet that they too had been made to feel like outsiders by society. Not that this was an excuse to engage in criminal activity or violence, though he could understand the frustration that might've fuelled it. Just his rotten luck one of the robbers had worn a bear mask. Why couldn't he have chosen something else—like a gorilla or even a duck?

Thelonious had locked away his camera gear in the Mini's boot to resist the temptation to stop and take more photos. His work here was done. As for what came next, he wasn't so sure. Perhaps another book if his publisher still wanted to work with him, especially after all this. He had time left on his visa. America was a big place—he could pitch a few ideas to Ira. In the meantime he tried to enjoy the country air blowing in through the car windows, though it no longer smelled as sweet as it once did.

As he crossed the state line into Tennessee, Thelonious

found himself welcomed by a familiar blood-spattered billboard. Apparently the fake-tanned, snake-loving Pastor Jehoshaphat Jones had yet another revival meeting up his dodgy sleeve. Was there no escaping these loonies?

When he saw the Mini Cooper approaching from the opposite lane, Thelonious's mouth pulled into a wide grin, delighted by this unexpected appearance of a kindred spirit. However, his delight quickly turned to disappointment when he realised it was one of those copy-cat foreign jobs. Upon seeing the individual behind the steering wheel, Thelonious's disappointment turned to disbelief.

The car was being driven by a chicken.

A goat occupied the passenger seat, and it was puffing away on a big cigar. The acrid stench found its way into the Mini and subsequently into Thelonious's nostrils, lodging in his throat like ground-up glass. As the two vehicles came parallel with each other, the rear window suddenly whirred down. A pig and a bear were sitting in the back seat.

Thrusting a short arm out the window toward Thelonious, the bear stuck its middle-finger in the air.

About the Authors

Mitzi Szereto (mitziszereto.com) is an author and anthology editor of multi-genre fiction. She has her own blog, Errant Ramblings: Mitzi Szereto's Weblog and a Web TV channel, Mitzi TV, which covers "quirky" London, England. Her books include *Normal for Norfolk (The Thelonious T. Bear Chronicles)*; *Florida Gothic*; *Oysters and Pearls: Collected Stories*; *The Wilde Passions of Dorian Gray*; *Pride and Prejudice: Hidden Lusts*; *Getting Even: Revenge Stories*; *Dying For It: Tales of Sex and Death*; *Thrones of Desire: Erotic Tales of Swords, Mist and Fire*; *Red Velvet and Absinthe*; *Love, Lust and Zombies* and other titles. Her anthology *Erotic Travel Tales 2* is the first anthology of erotica to feature a Fellow of the Royal Society of Literature. She divides her time between England and the USA. Find her on Twitter and Facebook.

Teddy Tedaloo (teddytedaloo.com) is co-author of *The*

Thelonious T. Bear Chronicles novels, including *Normal for Norfolk (The Thelonious T. Bear Chronicles).* A celebrity teddy bear, trendsetter and world traveller, he's also the publisher and editor of the online newspaper *The Teddy Tedaloo Times* and the production assistant extraordinaire/co-star of Mitzi TV. Popular in social media circles such as Twitter and Facebook, he's known for his entertaining commentary as well as being an animal welfare advocate. He lives (and goes) wherever Mitzi lives (and goes). *Rotten Peaches* is his second novel in the cosy mystery series featuring ursine protagonist Thelonious T. Bear.

Be sure to watch for more books in *The Thelonious T. Bear Chronicles* series!